DEAR CHARLOTTE

SUSAN M VIEMEISTER

Cover design by Susan M Viemeister

Edited by Maggie Bradbury

TO READ. FOR ALWAYS BEING THERE.

CONTENTS

	Acknowledgments	i
1	Chapter One	1
2	Chapter Two	5
3	Chapter Three	20
4	Chapter Four	24
5	Chapter Five	26
6	Chapter Six	32
7	Chapter Seven	39
8	Chapter Eight	44
9	Chapter Nine	47
10	Chapter Ten	51
11	Chapter Eleven	58
12	Chapter Twelve	78
13	Chapter Thirteen	83
14	Chapter Fourteen	96
15	Chapter Fifteen	99
16	Chapter Sixteen	108
17	Chapter Seventeen	114
18	Chapter Eighteen	117
19	Chapter Nineteen	120
20	Chapter Twenty	133

21   Chapter Twenty-One   141

22   Chapter Twenty-Two   152

23   Chapter Twenty-Three   168

24   Chapter Twenty-Four   172

25   Chapter Twenty-Five   179

ACKNOWLEDGMENTS

There were times I didn't know if this book would ever see the light of day. I started writing this story in 2009 and there were many interruptions along the way. Having said that, there are a few people whose contributions made this story happen. I want to thank former investigator Chuck Reid, Bedford County Sheriff's Office, for his knowledge, experience and expertise on crime scenes. Here's to ponies and unicorns. Also, Kristin Rosser, for inspiring a character that would pull this story together- what are friends for? My husband Read, for being behind me and encouraging me, ok, pushing me, to finish this story. And Great Aunt Charlotte Viemeister. Though I never knew you, your postcards got my imagination flowing. Thank you.

1 CHAPTER ONE

Dear Charlotte,

Merry Christmas & Happy New Year. We are having a lot of snow and cold here. The other day it was 16 below zero. Cold enough. How is the weather where you are now? I sent your address to Leon who is in Paris. Am still in Montreal, expect to stay here for the winter.

Yours expressly,

Hubert

Dear Charlotte,

There is just no other place like Paris.

Love

Pacha

Dear Charlotte,

Now don't forget to send me your address when you get to Europe, and send me some cards. I will not forget you-write and I will answer.

Yours,

Adam

Dear Miss Charlotte,

Will be glad to receive a few cards from you occasionally.

Leon

My Dear Charlotte,

Why do you not answer?? Please do so, as quick as possible I hope you are not angry with contents of my letter.

Best regards yours,

Brother

Charlotte,

I never forget what I promise.

Edwardo

Dear sister Charlotte,

Mother is home ten days & hasn't heard from you. She is anxiously

2

expecting a letter.

Your money sent off yesterday.

Brother

Dear Miss Charlotte,

There is a long time I had news from you that I believe you forgot me altogether.

Hope to have a card from you before the end of the week. Because I would not get to see you next week, thinking to have done something wrong to you.

Yours very sincerely,

Henri

Dear Miss Charlotte,

I like you,

Like your smile,

I like your style,

That twinkle in your eye,

I can't say why,

Hip Hip Hooray

Marcel

My Darling Charlotte,

I haven't heard from you how is this? Hope I will get a letter today. Will leave Paris for Boulogne Sur Mer on Saturday Oct 6 at 8:25 am. I went to Notre Dame yesterday. I thought of Victor Hugo. Good by dear Charlotte.

B.

Dear momma,

I am glad that you have returned from your visit to me again. I shall try to be a good girl.

Your daughter,

Charlotte

2 CHAPTER TWO

"Dammit dog! Slow down! You know I can't run as fast as you can!" Holly yelled as her Pointer, Rocket, ran ahead. Holly and Rocket were out on their run along a wooded trail that had once been part of an old railroad, but had long since been abandoned. Still, the trail was used by hikers, runners, and more recently, mountain bikers looking for a place to get away from the overcrowded park trails. It was a beautiful June morning in Virginia, with the temperature already close to 80 degrees, and promising to climb much higher. Holly's legs burned as the trail started its uphill climb. She tried to keep an eye out for rocks and roots that she might trip on. Luckily, even though the trail wound its way uphill for the next several miles, it was also going through a nicely wooded section. At least the trees were providing some welcome shade in the climbing heat. As she ran along, Holly concentrated on what a gorgeous day it was, and how beautiful the woods were, with all the wildflowers scattered throughout the woods and along the trails. Coming upon a bunch of daffodils growing along the trail, Holly briefly wondered how they got there. There were no traces of old houses that she could see. Who could have planted them there? She always wondered about stuff like that, it was interesting to think of what the area had been like years ago when the railway was operating. Those thoughts also helped keep her mind off how hard she was breathing now, how hot she was and how tired her legs felt. Only a little further and they would be at the top. Then it was a nice winding downhill run through the woods to the creek, where they would run along the creek for a while, before the trail climbed again, and then looped back down to the parking area. Reaching the top, a nice breeze started up and Holly breathed a little easier. "Man, that breeze feels good." she said. Rocket was panting pretty hard now too, his tongue lolling out his mouth. Taking a drink from her water bottle, they wound their way down to the creek, where Holly figured they could stop and let him play in the water to cool off.

"Rocket, come back here!" Holly called as Rocket suddenly ran off the trail, disappearing into the brush along the side. She could just barely see him, the liver colored ticking on his white coat blended in with foliage. Holly whistled again and Rocket came bounding back to her, carrying something in his mouth.

"I sure hope that's not a dead animal," she said as she got closer and the smell of something dead hit her. "Now drop it, and let's get back to our run, we don't have all day." Holly's annoyance with her dog's misbehavior turned to horror however, when she looked at what had been dropped before her. It was a shoe, with the partial remains of a human leg and foot still in it.

* * *

Detective Parker Williams pulled his car into the parking lot and stopped at the entrance to the trail. Noting the deputies and emergency workers already at the scene, Parker got out of his car and approached the deputies. "Who found the body?" he asked as he walked up to them.

"Woman with the dog over there talking to Ricky," replied AJ Rice, one of the deputies. "Said she was running when the dog took off into the brush and came out with a shoe, still had a foot in it. She looked where the dog came out of and saw the rest of the body. Appears to have been there a little while, we're waiting on the Medical Examiner now."

AJ saw Parker glance toward the ambulance parked nearby. "Don't worry she's not on today." Parker realized he had been holding his breath and slowly let it out. Karen, his ex, was a paramedic with the rescue squad. Their breakup had not been amicable, and running into her on the job was generally not a pleasant experience.

"How far up the trail is it?" Parker asked AJ.

"From here about a mile. We got some four wheelers on the way since we can't get the cars through at this end. There is an access road, but you have to drive about five miles up the road to get to it. Unless you prefer to walk." Parker looked at AJ, who at 5 foot 10 and 300 pounds didn't walk much if he could help it, then started walking towards the trail. Parker, in his mid-thirties, 6 feet tall and 160 pounds, his dark brown hair cut short, could still pass for a Marine. He prided himself on staying in shape by running, cycling and regular visits to the gym. It didn't take him long to reach the area where the body was found. As a deputy marked off with yellow crime scene tape, Parker took in the scene as he

7

approached. The body was that of a woman in her sixties, fully clothed and lying face down. She appeared to have severe head trauma, the right arm was missing from the elbow down, and the right leg was missing from just below the ankle. The body had started decomposing, and was bloating in the heat.

Parker walked up to another detective at the scene. Kenny Mann had been a detective for over 10 years. About the same height as Parker, but carrying about 20 pounds more, Kenny was also an avid mountain bike rider and the two had ridden the trails around the area together many times.

"What have we got?" Parker asked Kenny.

"It looks like someone was pretty angry, considering the head trauma. We'll need the autopsy results of course, but I would say it's pretty obvious the head injuries are what killed her. Jesus, I haven't seen anything like this before. I doubt her own family would recognize her. From the way she's dressed, it appears she may have been hiking. Once the ME gets here, we can check for any ID. Otherwise, we don't have a whole lot so far, doesn't seem like much of a struggle. Figure she probably was hit from behind, and had no idea what happened. The murder weapon appears to be that rock over there. We also found a walking stick nearby. Whoever did it actually broke it, and it's pretty solid. Breaking it wouldn't have been easy. We've got someone checking on the vehicles in the parking lot, we identified her car there. We'll have it taken in so forensics can go over it. "

Parker nodded. "I spoke to Jim Nichols. He said he can't make it to the scene, so we don't have to hold anything up for him." The Commonwealth Attorney was well known to be a stickler for crime scene protocol. Normally the detectives would wait for him to arrive before anyone moved the body.

The police photographer signaled he was done, and Parker and Kenny approached the body. Kenny turned at the sound of someone approaching. "Well, here comes the ME."

Kate Spade was walking towards the detectives. Tall, thin, and beautiful, her blond hair done in a stylish bob that fell to her jawbone, Kate was often mistaken for a model. Smart and soft spoken, she was well liked by the detectives. Her looks and easy going manner bellied a tough as nails attitude, she didn't tolerate laziness or sloppiness when it came to her cases. Parker and Kate had been out for dinner several times, which hadn't gone over well with Karen, who, despite the breakup, still held out hope she and Parker would reconcile.

"Hey Kate," Kenny said.

"Hi guys," she replied, nodding at Parker as she set her bag down and kneeled by the body. "Man, this is a bad one. I'd say she's been here for a few days at least, and it looks like the animals have gotten to her. From what I can tell so far, the head trauma seems to be the only trauma. I don't see any other obvious signs of death, but I won't know for sure until she's back at the morgue and I've got her on the table." Kate took several photos herself, and examined the front of the body, before rolling it over and examining the back. Checking the pockets of the woman's pants, Kate pulled out a wallet. Pulling out the driver's license, she handed it to Parker, who read it and handed it to Kenny.

"Well, that answers one mystery," Kenny said. "Charlotte Phillips-Pierce. Her family reported her missing yesterday. She has been missing for a couple of days."

"Nothing like living in a small town," Parker responded. "Let's hope we can solve the murder that fast."

"I hear you. This is one you don't forget. She's a rich woman, well known around town. The son that reported her missing is a mountain biker, too. I've bumped into him and his wife out on the trails."

"Do we have all the parts?" Kate asked Parker.

"Yes. We have a shoe with her right foot and part of her right leg, the arm is over here. I want to bag her hands before she gets moved in case there is any DNA under her nails. It doesn't look like she put up a struggle, but with the condition the body is in, it's hard to tell."

Kate and the two detectives looked up at the same time to see the turkey vultures starting to circle. "I guess we found her just in time, I hate it when they get to the body first."

"Got that right," replied Kenny as he started placing the paper bags on the victim's hands. Pretty soon they had everything bagged and ready to go. The morgue van was parked at the trail head, so Kenny and Parker assisted the driver with carrying the stretcher back down the trail and to the van.

"When will you be doing the post?" Parker asked Kate.

"Probably later this afternoon, depending on what is waiting for me when I get back. The condition the body is in, I'd prefer to do it sooner than later. I'm also sure you're anxious for any clues that might come up since it appears we have a killer on the loose. Are you coming in to watch?"

"I'm going to try, but first I need to talk to her son. I'll check in with you after I talk to him, see where we're at. Kenny, are you going to watch the post as well?"

Kenny didn't relish the idea of watching the autopsy, the crime scene was bad enough, and at the autopsy's he had attended in the past, he had thrown up and passed out. It had been embarrassing to say the least, and certainly not the image he wanted to portray as the tough detective he was.

"I'll pass," he replied, wiping the sweat from his forehead. "I want to start checking into her background, see what I can find out. Let me know if you come up with anything after talking to the son. See where we go from there."

"OK, I'm going to head over there now. I'll check in with you and Kate before I leave there." With that, Parker got into his car and called in for the address of the son. As he turned the car around and started heading to the given address, Parker sighed. Man, how he hated this part. Telling someone that a loved one had been killed was never easy. You knew that their lives would never be the same. At the same time, you never knew if you were talking to the killer, either. Quite often the killer turned out to be a family member, so the detective knew he had to keep his mind open to everything and anything. Driving along Parker thought how ironic it was that it was such a glorious day, people were no doubt out enjoying the weather, and yet here he was, heading out to deliver some horrible news to someone.

Stella had just finished her ride and was walking her Pinto gelding back to the barn when the dogs started barking. Looking to see what all the commotion was about, she noticed the unmarked car pulling up the driveway of the small farm. Stopping at the gate, Stella waited on the car to park and the driver to get out.

"Are you Stella Pierce?" Parker asked

"Yes, can I help you?"

"Is your husband around? I'll need to talk to him."

"He should be right up, he was riding his bike on the trail," Stella had a sinking feeling in her stomach, if the cops are here, it can't be good. "Is this about his mom?"

"Yes, I'm afraid she's dead," Parker replied, watching closely for any reaction.

"Oh crap. What happened? Did she have a heart attack, stroke, car accident?"

Parker hesitated before replying, "It appears she's been murdered."

"Murdered? Are you kidding? How? What happened?" Stella shook her head. "I can't believe it. Hang on, let me put the horse away and I'll find Graham."

Parker watched Stella untack her horse and turn him back out in the field. Stella was an attractive, fit brunette in her thirties. As Stella rejoined Parker in the driveway, Graham rode up out the woods behind the barn on his mountain bike. "Nice bike," Parker noted, "haven't I seen you out on the trails on Stony Mountain?"

"Yeah, I thought I recognized you," Graham said. "Graham Pierce," he said, shaking hands with Parker. Graham was the same height and build as Parker, very fit, late thirties, good looking with dark eyes and dark brown hair. "Let me guess, the old lady is dead."

"Yes, how did you know?" Parker replied.

"I have a keen sense of the obvious. She's been missing and now there is a cop in my driveway. What happened?"

"It appears she was murdered. She was found on the trails over by the old railroad. A woman running with her dog found her. She had some pretty severe head trauma."

Graham looked surprised. "Murdered?"

"Couldn't it have been an accident, like a fall?" Stella asked.

"No, it was definitely not an accident, though we will need to wait on the autopsy to be sure," replied Parker as the image of the crime scene flooded in his mind. "Do you have any idea of who would want to kill your mother?"

"It'd be easier to ask who wouldn't," Graham said. When Parker looked at him, Graham continued, "I guess you never met her. According to her, she was a saint, and I'm sure you'll find people who will tell you how kind and generous she was. However, she was crazy. She was incredibly difficult to be around, depending on her mood. She wouldn't listen to anything you told her, she always knew better than you. She was so afraid of looking stupid she would never admit she didn't know something. I was always trying to look out for her to make sure she wasn't being taken advantage of. If she found out I was trying to protect her, she became angry because I didn't trust her judgment. Or thought she couldn't take care of herself. She could be totally impossible to deal with. It wouldn't surprise me if she pissed off the wrong person, had a jealous lover, or promised to leave her money to someone. She did that all the time. Or it could have been the ax murderer, though I think he's still locked up. She was afraid of him getting paroled."

"Ax murderer?" Parker was astounded.

"Yeah, it was the grounds-keeper's son who, in a drug fueled rage, hacked his girlfriend to death up in Connecticut about 20 years ago. Mom decided she was going to be supportive of this kid because she liked the family. I told her she should be supportive to the people who lost their daughter, but that's the way she is. She's been writing and sending this guy money all this time while he's been in prison, never thinking about what would happen when he got out. Now he's up for parole, and has been telling her he wants to come live with her."

"What is his name? And you said he hasn't been paroled yet?"

"Kevin Whitman and I don't believe he's out. He was turned down a number of times because he's absolutely nuts, but who knows. And you can't believe anything the old lady tells you, everything she says is either a lie or some fantasy of hers."

"I'll have to check on Kevin. Is there anyone else that comes to mind?"

"Like I said, it could be anybody. She could be very generous with her money, and people took advantage. In the guise of helping them, she would pay their mortgage, put kids through college, funnel money into their business, whatever, depending on who she was trying to impress. She was very needy emotionally and fed off the attention she got when she did stuff like that. It was also her way of controlling people."

"When was the last time you saw or spoke to your mother?" Parker asked.

Graham thought for a minute and said, "Last Wednesday. Her lawn mower wouldn't start, and I stopped by to fix it. Because of her age, I usually drove by to make sure everything at least looked ok. Her car was there the next morning when I drove by, but that's the last time I saw her. My sister called Sunday morning to ask if mom was ok because they talked every day and she hadn't heard from her, and couldn't get her on the phone. I went by the house. and when I didn't see the car, I stopped in and looked. It looked like she hadn't been there for a while, so I called the police. I thought maybe she had gotten into a wreck or something."

"She lived alone?" Parker asked.

"Yes." Graham replied.

Parker was still making notes when he turned to Stella. "What about you? When was the last time you saw Charlotte?" he asked.

"I'm not sure of the exact day," Stella replied. "I tried to avoid her whenever I could. I think it was about a month or so ago. We stopped over there on the way out to dinner. I'm pretty sure that was the last time."

Turning again to Graham, Parker asked "Can you tell me where you've been and what you've done for the last week?"

"Am I a suspect?" Graham asked.

15

"Right now everyone is a suspect. It's pretty standard when doing a murder investigation. We need to start ruling people out, that's why I'm asking you these questions. Once we eliminate someone as a suspect we can go on with the investigation."

Graham didn't look convinced, but said he had nothing to hide. "I've been working. I'm an investment broker. My partner and I have been pretty busy with that for the past 2 weeks. When I'm done for the day, I usually come home and do stuff around the farm. The past 3 days after work I've gone riding at Stony Mountain. I'm trying to get ready for race next month."

Parker turned to Stella. "Can you tell me where you were the past several days, too, please?"

"I've pretty much been here at the farm working with the horses. One of them was sick the other morning and I've been hanging around to take care of him. Let's see, I also went riding with Graham the day before yesterday and did some grocery shopping yesterday, but I got back here around eleven, I guess. After Graham came home we went for a ride. "

"Where do your siblings live?" Parker asked Graham.

"Jake and his family live in New York. Ellen and her latest husband live in Richmond, and Emily lives outside Lynchburg."

"And your mother lived nearby here, is that correct?"

"Yes, she lives a few miles from here, on Stony Hollow Rd. She moved here about 10 years ago. She used to come visit us here and loved the area. After my sisters moved here, I guess she felt the need to be near family, and to be perfectly honest, I don't think anyone else wanted her near them. So she came here."

"What about your brother, didn't you say he still lived in New York?"

"Yeah, but they don't get along. Like I said, Mom can be incredibly difficult to deal with. She is very spoiled and manipulative. One minute she's caring, interested in you, wanting to help you out if she can. Then she's bitching at you, making you feel like shit while she lavishes love on someone else. She's ruined a number of people's lives, besides her own kids. Yet we still keep trying to get her to love us, be a mother, you know? Jake probably has the hardest time with it. He never got over the divorce and the shit that went down afterwords. Oh yeah, Jonathan is living in Michigan now, I think. I don't keep up with him, so I'm not positive."

"Jonathan?"

"He's the son she had after the divorce. We don't deal with him much; he's the golden child that can do no wrong. The way Mom has always treated him you would think he could walk on water. The reality is, he's a spoiled, lazy brat who uses Mom to bail him out of whatever mess he managed to get into. He's always giving some sob story and she just goes along with it. It's pathetic."

Parker had been jotting down notes as Graham talked, "She sounds like quite a character."

Graham shook his head. "You have no idea."

"What else can you tell me about her? You mentioned jealous lovers. Did she have a boyfriend?"

"At the moment I don't know of anyone. Mom was drop

dead gorgeous in her day, and still quite attractive. Men were always falling for her. Her parents were quite wealthy and rumor has it when mom was young she got involved with a married man. To avoid a scandal that would taint the family, her parents sent her to school in Switzerland. Mom basically grew up in Europe, traveling all over and living quite a life. A few years ago I found a box of old postcards written to her while she was living in Europe. They were mostly from men. She must have been quite popular. I know her parents didn't really know how to handle her. She was beautiful, rich, spoiled and on her own over there. You know, I don't know what happened to her that made her so crazy. When I talk to people that knew her when she was young, she wasn't like this at all. It's like they are describing a totally different person. Whatever happened, it's still a secret, and I guess now we'll never know."

"Any other relatives, family?"

"Oh yeah, she has a brother, half- brother actually, Charles. He lives in Connecticut. I haven't talked to him in years, but I probably have his number here somewhere if you need it."

Parker put his notebook away. "Thank you, if you could give me a call when you find his number, I may or may not need to talk to him. With these cases you never know. Normally, we would have you come down and make a formal ID on the body, but unfortunately, I don't think that will be. possible in this case. We will probably need to go by dental records. Do you know who her dentist was?"

Graham was feeling a bit ill thinking of what Parker just said. The reality was starting to sink in. "She went to Dr. Bishop," he said.

"Ok, we'll contact him for her records. I'm really sorry about your mom. I may have more questions as we do our investigation. Meanwhile, if you think of anything that might help, no matter how trivial it may seem, please give me a call," Parker said as he handed a business card to Graham.

"Thanks," said Graham. "We'll do that. Please keep us informed of what is going on and I hope you find who did this quickly."

"Don't worry. I will do everything in my power to find the killer. I won't stop, no matter how long it takes." With that Parker nodded goodbye and got in his car. Both Graham and Stella looked shaken. Putting their arms around each other, they turned and headed into the house. Sighing, Parker drove slowly down the drive, and headed for the morgue.

Parker thought about his interview with Graham and Stella as he headed to meet Kate at the morgue. He had an uneasy feeling about this case. This was going to be a difficult one he thought as he drove along. If what he learned from Graham and Stella was any indication, talking to the other siblings should be interesting, to say the least. He wondered if they all had the same feelings about their mother. Jake sounded like he had a lot of anger towards his mother, was it enough to kill her? He would also have to check out the will, see who would benefit from her death. And what about Graham? He lived nearby, and was used to the trails from mountain biking. He was certainly strong enough to kill her. And Stella? She admitted she avoided her mother-in-law, what had happened between them to make her feel that way? Not to mention the ax murderer. What kind of woman had Charlotte been? Parker had a feeling he didn't really want to find out.

3 CHAPTER THREE

Victor Pierce stood before his four young children. Tall, blond, with a chiseled face, a bit heavier than his days on the college rowing team; Victor towered over the children, Jake 12, Graham 10, Ellen, 8 and Emily, 6. "Ok kids, your mother and I have decided to separate. You will be staying with your mother, and I'll be moving out. I just want you to know I love you all, and will still see you and be part of your lives."

"But Dad, why can't you stay?" Ellen started crying, "We don't want you to go!" The other kids started protesting as well, but they were cut off by Victor.

"Now stop it. I don't want to go, either. But sometimes these things happen. I want you to mind your mother. I'll see you on the weekends and holidays. Also, your mother agrees you will be going to boarding school. There is a good school in New Hampshire that you will be attending next year. "

"But Dad! We don't want to go away to school, we like our school here!" Jake cried.

"Now Jake, it's already been decided. You're going, and it will be all right. You'll like it there. Now give me a hug, I have to get going now, and you guys need to go to bed." The boys each hugged Victor, while

Ellen and her little sister Emily were almost inconsolable and didn't want to let go. Finally, Victor peeled the girls off him, put them down and left. After his car started up, Charlotte came into the room. Slim and petite, waist length blond hair and large blue eyes, Charlotte carried herself with an aristocratic air. One of only two children of wealthy parents, Charlotte was born on the "Gold Coast" of Long Island, attending the finest schools and living in various homes that most people would consider mansions, with nannies, servants and chauffeurs. "Ok now, time for bed. Boys, get going. Girls, stop crying, and come on."

"Mom, why is Dad leaving?"

"Your father and I are not getting along. It has nothing to do with you. We are going to live apart for a while. Now, enough questions go to bed."

"What about the boarding school, we don't want to go," the children started crying again.

"You're going to the school and that is all there is to it. Don't make this harder that it is. And don't make me tell you again to get to bed!"

The kids knew that they better listen, and headed off to bed. "This sucks, how can he just leave like that?" Jake angrily asked Graham.

"I know, what are we going to do?" Graham replied.

"I don't know yet, but I know I sure don't want to go away to any freaking boarding school!" Jake responded.

"Me neither," Graham said. Jake stormed into his room and slammed the door. Graham was worried about his older brother. Jake had a hair trigger temper, and you never knew what he would do. Graham had been on the receiving end of Jake's temper on more than one occasion, and had learned to tread carefully around his moods. He could

still hear his sisters crying in their room. Ellen was especially devastated, having been the closest to their father.

Later, when Charlotte checked on the children, none of them said a word. "Goodnight," Charlotte softly told each of them as she went from room to room. After Charlotte left the girls room, Lady, the family's sable colored Collie padded into the room. Going up to Ellen, Lady started licking her face.

"Oh Lady, what would I do without you?" Ellen cried as she wrapped her arms around Lady's neck, burying her face in Lady's soft fur.

"Get out of the car you two, now!"

"Mom! What are you talking about? Come on, we're going to be late getting back to school!" Jake yelled.

"Get out of the car Goddammit! NOW! Move it!" Charlotte yelled back.

"What did we do?" Graham was freaking out. Charlotte was supposed to be driving them back to the boarding school they were attending in New Hampshire, and now she was throwing them out of the car on the side of the highway.

"I said get out of the God damn car, now! I don't have time for this!" Charlotte was screaming at the boys. Jake and Graham grabbed their suitcases and got out, as Charlotte stomped on the gas and took off, leaving her young sons on the side of the highway.

"What the hell is with her? We are going to be so screwed showing up late," Jake fumed. At 13, he was already quite tall for his age, and

being the oldest assumed responsibility for his younger brother. "I guess we try and hitch a ride. Hopefully we'll get there before we get in too much trouble for being late. That bitch. I wish Dad would get custody like he's been trying to do. Maybe when he hears about this latest bullshit of hers, we can go live with him."

"I think she's in a hurry to get back to her boyfriend," answered Graham.

"What are you talking about? What boyfriend?" Jake replied as he attempted to flag down a ride from the passing motorists.

"Marcus, he's the latest one. Don't tell me you're too stoned all the time now to notice," Graham said. "She's always got some guy "friend" coming over. Yeah, right. I caught her and Marcus making out last night. She doesn't know I saw her. "

"No shit! Damn, maybe I am too stoned all the time," laughed Jake as a car pulled over. "Does Dad know about this? Maybe it will help with the custody case. That would be cool. I don't know how much more of her bullshit and moods I can take. I swear that woman is freaking crazy. I'll bet Granddad Phillips would love to hear about this, too. He's trying to help Dad with the custody case. Come on little brother, let's get going, I don't know what we're going to tell the headmaster, I don't think they'll believe us if we say Mom left us on the side of the road. And you know her, if they call her, she'll say we're lying anyway. Stupid, crazy bitch."

4 CHAPTER FOUR

"How can the courts allow her to keep the kids, when she's so irresponsible?" Victor was livid. "Did you hear the latest lunacy on her part? The house was on the courthouse steps, they were going to foreclose on it because she wasn't paying the mortgage! It's not like she doesn't have the money, it was just too much of a bother to pay it! And they let her retain custody?"

Victor paced back and forth as he yelled into the phone. On the other end was his former father-in-law, Thomas Phillips.

"I know, it is insane and doesn't make any sense. But the courts don't like to take children away from their mother, no matter how crazy she is. I'm really sorry about this Victor. I'm not sure what else we can do at this point."

Victor ran his hand through his hair as he stopped pacing momentarily. "Back when I told you I was going to ask Charlotte to marry me, you told me not to. I remember you said she was spoiled, crazy, and would ruin my life. At the time I thought that was such a horrible thing for a father to say about his own daughter. I decided I was going to ride up on my white horse and rescue her from her father. Now I see what you meant, and you were right. It was a mistake to get married. I don't think anyone would be able to deal with her. The only good thing I got out of it is my kids, and I can barely see them thanks to her shenanigans."

Thomas sighed into the phone. "I remember that conversation, too. I knew you thought I was being too harsh, but I've always liked you, and didn't want to see you get hurt. I thought maybe it would work out for you and was sad to hear you were divorcing. I'll have another talk with her. She is being utterly selfish and needs to start thinking about those kids she is supposed to care so much about. I hate to have to cut her out of the will, but it may come to that. I may need to leave it to the children and not her. At least that way I could rest knowing they would be protected. God knows Charlotte doesn't have a clue about finance."

Victor was still shaking with fury as he hung up the phone. There had to be a way to get his kids back, this just couldn't go on.

Charlotte looked at her plate. A few minutes ago the eggs she had fixed for breakfast had looked and smelled delicious. Now suddenly she felt ill. I wonder if I'm coming down with something she thought as she dumped the eggs in the dog bowl. Lady trotted over to the bowl and delicately ate the eggs. After licking the bowl clean she sat and looked hopefully at Charlotte. "I hope you enjoyed them but don't get your hopes up for any more it's strictly dog food from here on out." With a sigh, Lady got up and walked out of the room. Suddenly Charlotte ran to the bathroom as the feeling of nausea overwhelmed her. After, she washed her face and sat down on the edge of the tub. "Oh no,no,no." she moaned as she realized what was wrong. Putting her face in her hands, Charlotte started to sob.

5 CHAPTER FIVE

"Ok kids, come on. We're going to be late." Charlotte was taking the children to visit her father at his house on the water. The kids loved going there. The house was on a small bluff overlooking Long Island Sound, surrounded by 40 acres of fields and woods, horses to ride, the beach to run on, swimming, fishing and boating, it was a kid's paradise. Lady ran around the kids, barking and trying to herd them towards the car.

"Look Mom, Lady knows where we're going, too!" Ellen said as she got in the car, Lady bounding in after her.

"I'm sure she does, honey," Charlotte responded, "Now let's get going. Is everyone in? We're on our way". The kids chattered excitedly as they drove along, talking about all the things they were going to do at their grandfather's place. Jake was already bragging about the fish he would catch and cook for dinner, which elicited comments from his siblings on his lack of fishing skills and how they would all starve.

"Yeah, well, just see if I share them with you," Jake responded.

"Considering the size of the last fish you caught, you couldn't share it if you tried," laughed Graham.

"Well, you just wait and see. At least I can catch something. When was the last time you hooked a fish, huh?"

"Ok boys, settle down, no more arguing," Charlotte said as she drove along. She could see this was soon going to enter into full blown bickering if they didn't find something else to talk about. The last thing she needed today was listening to the kids argue. "I sure hope Dad doesn't make me go on the boat," she thought, "I don't think I could stand it today."

"Mom, are we going to be able to ride today?" Emily asked, "Will you ride with me?"

"I don't know sweetheart, we'll have to see once we get there. Maybe your sister will ride with you."

"But Mom, we always ride together!" Emily protested.

"Emily, I said we would see once we got there, now drop it!" Charlotte's mood was worsening and they hadn't even gotten to the house yet. Emily and her sister exchanged looks, Ellen rolling her eyes. Charlotte's mood swings were getting more frequent and they never knew when she would blow up on them. They lowered their voices and whispered between them.

"What a bitch," Jake muttered. "I hope she's not going to be this way the whole day."

"It'll be fine once we get there, we'll just stay out of the house and let Grandfather deal with her," Graham replied.

"Maybe we can get her to take the boat out and let it float out to sea," Jake said, setting the girls to giggling.

"Isn't that what happened to her first husband? He supposedly *drowned after falling off of their yacht?" Graham whispered.*

"Yeah, that's the story I've always been told. It was an accident. Maybe he jumped because he couldn't take her moods anymore." replied Jake.

"Or maybe she pushed him," snickered Graham.

"What's going on back there?" Charlotte asked.

"Nothing," the kids replied at once, then breaking into more laughter.

Charlotte gritted her teeth and drove faster.

Once at her father's house, the kids and dog piled out of the car and ran towards their grandfather. Thomas gave each of them a hug, and then they were off, running to the beach. Charlotte got out and walked up to her father. Noticing his stern expression as he watched her approach, she tried a smile.

"Oh, hi," she said as she approached her father. "The kids have been so excited about coming out, it's all they've been talking about all week."

"Hi Charlotte," Thomas replied dryly, "It's always nice to have the kids here. It's even nicer when you bring them when I'm here, too, instead of showing up when I'm away. How are you doing? You look pale, are you feeling ok?"

"I'm fine, just a touch of something I guess. I don't know when you're here or not, I just bring the kids when I can," Charlotte answered defensively.

"We need to talk. Come inside with me." Thomas said as he turned toward the house. Charlotte paused a moment before following. "This couldn't be good, she thought", her mood darkening, "It's probably some

crap Victor is feeding him, trying to get Thomas on his side to gain custody of the kids." Once inside the house, Charlotte followed her father into the library, closing the door behind her. Normally the library was a comfort to her, the smell of the books and the leather chairs always made her feel good. However, today there was a different mood in the room.

"Victor called." Thomas looked at his daughter. "He said the house was nearly foreclosed on. What is going on, why haven't you been paying the mortgage?"

Charlotte started pacing the room. "It's no big deal. I was just busy and forgot to pay. It's all settled now, so Victor doesn't have to worry. It's not his house anyway." Thomas stared at his daughter.

"It is a big deal. If you lost the house because you were too "busy" to pay the mortgage, you and your children would be out on the street. What the hell is wrong with you? How can you be so self-centered that you would put your children in a situation like that?" Thomas yelled. "I'm also hearing stories of how they are left alone while you're out running around all over town with your boyfriends. You are supposed to be raising these kids, not letting them raise themselves!"

"Is that what Victor is telling you? He's making it up just to try and make me look bad so. he can get custody. Well he's not getting them, they are mine!" Charlotte yelled back.

"You don't care about those kids, you just want to punish Victor for the divorce, even though you were the one that wanted out of the marriage."

"That's not true! I love my children, everyone knows that, how can you say that to me?" Charlotte was beside herself. This was worse than she thought. Obviously Victor had her father on his side after all.

"Ignoring them while you run around satisfying all your desires, nearly losing your home, leaving them unattended all day or night, is hardly going to earn you Mother of the year awards." Thomas scowled. "Let me tell you one thing. If you don't start acting like a responsible adult, and less like a selfish, spoiled brat, I will help Victor gain custody. Don't think I won't, either."

Charlotte's face turned stormy. "What are you talking about? I take very good care of my kids! There is no reason I can't have a social life, either. Victor is just making this crap up to turn everyone against me so he can get custody. He doesn't want them, they might interfere with his new wife. He's just trying to ruin my life!" With that Charlotte turned and stormed out of the room. As she stomped down the hallway, Charlotte ran into her stepmother, Catherine. "Good morning Charlotte, it's good to see you. We're glad you came out to visit," Catherine said as she took Charlotte's hand in hers. Yanking her hand back, Charlotte swept by Catherine as she responded "Well, don't get too used to it, we're leaving now."

"What? Why are you leaving, you just got here?" Catherine asked.

"Ask your husband," was all Charlotte would say as she kept moving. Reaching the front door, Charlotte headed down the large yard toward the beach, where she could hear Lady barking and the shrieks of laughter of the children as they ran around the beach. Reaching the beach, Charlotte yelled for the children to come to her. "Come on, we're leaving now. Get you stuff and let's go!"

The girls were the first to hear her. "What's going on?" Ellen asked, "We just got here!"

"Get your stuff and get in the car, I said we're leaving." Charlotte grabbed Ellen's arm and turned for the house. Just then, Jake and

Graham came over.

"What's going on?" Graham asked.

"Mom said we have to leave," Emily cried. Jake turned angrily on his mother.

"What are you doing? You said we were going to stay all day, and now we have to leave? We just got here!"

"Don't take that tone with me, young man! Your grandfather doesn't want us here, get your things and let's go."

"That's bullshit! Grandfather said he was happy to see us, you're lying!" Jake yelled. With that Charlotte turned and slapped her oldest son across the face, stunning the other children into silence.

"Don't you dare talk to me like that! I'm your mother and you will NOT talk to me that way again, do you hear me?!" Charlotte's face was thunderous. Jake's eyes widened, then blinking back tears, face red, he watched as his mother grabbed Emily and Ellen and continued to the car. Graham looked terrified as he turned to his brother.

"Are you ok?" he asked.

"I hate that bitch!" Jake hissed. "Someday she'll be sorry, you just wait. She'll get hers one day," Jake muttered under his breath as they followed the others back to the car.

6 CHAPTER SIX

Parker's phone rang as he was pulling into the morgue. "Howdy, what's going on?" Porter "Squirrel" Stevens was a former SWAT team member of the police department and now worked as a Paranormal Investigator. "I hear you have an actual murder investigation on your hands. I didn't think there were murders in your neck of the woods."

Parker smiled as he responded, "Hey Squirrel, how did you hear about it already? Don't tell me things are so dull in the big city that you have to check out what's going on out here in the sticks."

"Nope, plenty of action here to keep us busy, lots of noises and things that go bump in the night, all that fun stuff. I just called the office to see how things were going and found out about your case. Have you got a suspect yet?"

Parker sighed. "No. I don't think this one is going to be easy," he replied as he started explaining the case to Squirrel. "I'm at the morgue now. I'm hoping Kate was able to find some evidence that might help. Right now we don't have a lot to go on. I've talked to one son and his wife, they live nearby. I'll be calling the other siblings and half-brother after I leave here, see what I can find out."

"If you need any help, let me know, it might be interesting to work a present day murder for a change. Most of the dead people I've been dealing with lately died in the last century. Speaking of Kate how is the lovely Dr. Spade? I hear she has designs on you, get it? Designs? Kate Spade, designer?"

"Funny. Don't give up your day job."

"I waste all my best material," Squirrel said. "By the way, Sarah wants to get together sometime."

"Tell Sarah sure, that sounds great. And she can even bring you if she wants." Parker laughed.

"Ha, I'll be sure to tell her. Anyway, I'll catch you later. Keep me posted, this sounds like a good one," Squirrel said.

"Will do. Or maybe I should just have you ask my victim who killed her," Parker laughed.

"That would be too easy, I want to see you solve this one the old fashioned way," Squirrel laughed back. "Go on and see what the beautiful ME has to say."

Kate was making the standard Y- incision on the body when Parker walked in. "Oh good, you're here," she said as he came up beside her. "So far the exterior only shows the head trauma, with a bruise on the top of the right shoulder. Looks like whoever killed her may have missed her head and hit her shoulder instead. There were no defensive wounds, no scratches or other bruising. No stray hairs or fibers found on the body. Nothing unusual on the clothes, either."

"Does the head injury appear to have been caused by the walking stick and rock we found?"

"Yes, I'll have the measurements in my report for you, but it was consistent with the size and shape of what you found at the scene. I'm sure when you get them back from forensics the blood will match. Hopefully there will be some prints on the stick since I don't think you'll find any on the rock."

"Yeah, I hope so, I'd like to get this one solved quickly. I have a feeling it's going to be a messy case." Parker watched as Kate examined and weighed all the organs before placing them back in the body.

"Well, overall she was pretty darn healthy, especially for her age. No sign of heart disease, lungs look good, liver and kidneys are fine. What a shame." Kate shook her head. " I'll wrap this up and get the report to you as soon as I can. Have you had anything to eat today? I was going to pick up something for dinner from Nicky's on the way home. You're welcome to join me."

"That sounds good to me. That's the Italian restaurant that just opened last month, isn't it?" Parker replied, "I'll bring the wine and meet you at your place at seven, if that works for you."

"Yes, they have great food there. Seven will be fine, let me finish up here and head out. I'll see you in a while." Parker couldn't help but smile as he left the morgue. Being around Kate just felt so right, especially after all the tension and drama with Karen. He still couldn't believe he ever got involved with her, what had he been thinking? The least he could have done was end it a lot sooner, but at the time he was pretty lonely, and Karen could be fun to be with, when she wasn't in one of her moods. *Oh well, I'm not going to think about that now,* he said to himself. *I have enough to worry about with this case.* Parker reached the car and smiled again as he got in and started it up. *Now, home to change and pick up the wine, and maybe a surprise for desert, then off to Kate's. A nice, romantic dinner was just what I needed after a day like today,* he thought.

Graham was on the phone with Jake. "Do they have any idea who killed her? " Jake was asking. "And what the hell was she doing out on some trail in the middle of nowhere at her age?" he said.

"No, not yet. And she was only sixty-seven, hardly ancient. This may surprise you, but people that age can be very active. Anyway, they just started the investigation. The detective said we needed to wait on the autopsy to be sure of how she died. Come on, you know your mother, she was always going off places by herself, you couldn't stop her. Remember the time she drove across the country by herself, because she wanted to go to Seattle? It doesn't surprise me at all she was out hiking. The only surprise is how she knew about that trail. It isn't that well known to anyone that is only a casual hiker. But then again, if she was trying to impress one of her new friends with how fit she was, I could see her out there."

"Yeah, I guess you're right. It's always what she wants to do, the hell with anyone else. I can just see her picking something remote knowing if she didn't turn up everyone would be looking for her. Then once again, she would be the center of attention, and show up acting like nothing is wrong and it's perfectly normal for a sixty-seven year old woman to be out by herself on some trail in the middle of nowhere. She's a freaking nutcase."

"Well, if that's the case, she got her wish because everyone was looking for her and now she is definitely the center of attention. I have to talk to Ellen and Emily. I'm sure they will be freaking out and if having your mother murdered wasn't bad enough, wait till they find out Mom left everything to Jonathan."

"Wait, what are you talking about?" Jake demanded on the other end of the phone. "The estate is split evenly between all of us!"

"No, it's not. I've seen copies of her will. Everything she has goes to Jonathan, we get nothing."

"Are you fucking kidding me?" Jake exploded. "That bitch! I don't believe this shit, why didn't you say something about this? Doesn't that just figure? She takes care of that self-absorbed leech, but leaves us nothing?" Graham held the phone away from his ear, as Jake continued on his tirade. There was no point in trying to reason with him when he was in this kind of mood. It was always better just to let him rant, and wait for him to calm down, before trying to say anything. After about fifteen minutes, Graham was finally able to get a word in.

"All right, look, enough about the will. There is nothing we can do about it, if you want to try and contest it, call a lawyer. I have other things to worry about, like funeral arrangements. Let me call the girls and let them know before they get a call from the cops. I'll keep you posted on any developments. Bye." Graham hung up the phone and groaned. His brother could be such an asshole. The last thing he needed right now was listening to Jake scream about the money and berate their mother. Yes, she was a pain in the ass, and incredibly self-centered, spoiled and difficult to deal with, but now she was dead. Murdered. *Give me a break already,* he thought, *I don't need this shit.* Just then Stella walked in the room. "Is it safe to come in? I could hear him yelling in the other room for God's sake. I take it he didn't take the news well."

"He didn't seem too rattled by her being killed, but man, he went off when I told him about the will. I guess that's all he's concerned about. Maybe once he thinks about it for a while it will sink in she's dead. I better get on the phone to Ellen and Emily before he does. Who knows what he'll end up saying."

"Is Jake going to call Jonathan?" Stella asked.

"I don't know, and quite frankly, I don't care. I wouldn't call that asshole even if I knew where he was or what his phone number is. He doesn't give a shit about mom anyway. He's always just been in it for the money. I can't believe she bought his act all these years, it's pathetic and sick. I've got a freaking headache now, and I still have to call the girls. Maybe I'll call Ellen and let her call Emily since I don't want to even think about this any longer."

"At least Emily won't be as bad as Jake. Of course, I think she may actually have cared about your mom. As far as Ellen, who knows what she really felt about her. I think she was another one full of lip service just to get the money. I'm sorry about your mom honey, can I get you anything?"

"No thanks. I better get this over with." Graham picked up the phone and dialed his sister's number.

Ellen was shaking as she hung up the phone. Mom murdered? It was a shock, but could she really say she was surprised? It's not like she never thought she'd get that phone call, the only surprise is that it didn't happen sooner. Her mind was whirling. This was going to be a huge mess. It seemed so surreal, her mom was always such a dominant force in her life, and now she was gone. Already Ellen could feel the emptiness where her mom once was in her life. Suddenly her cell phone rang. Noticing her sister Emily's number, Ellen answered.

7 CHAPTER SEVEN

Kate put the food she picked up from Nicky's in the oven to keep it warm, and then headed to the bathroom for a quick shower. As the hot water washed over her body, Kate thought about the upcoming dinner. After calling off her engagement two years ago, Kate had been leery of getting involved with anyone again, and threw herself into her work. Now here she was getting involved with a police detective, of all things. Was she making another mistake, she wondered, the last thing she needed was another heartbreak. But she was finding Parker hard to resist. With his good looks and easy going manner, Parker was easy to be with. Kate found herself feeling calmer just being in his presence.

"I hope I'm not making a mistake," she said out loud as she quickly dried her hair. Dressing in jeans and a dark green blouse that showed off her figure, Kate headed back to the kitchen and started setting the table. The doorbell rang as she was putting the wine on the table.

"Hey," Kate said as she opened the door, heart quickening as she looked at Parker. *Damn, he looks good,* she thought.

"Hey," Parker replied as he gave Kate a light kiss on her cheek. "You look great."

"Thanks," said Kate, "come in and make yourself at home."

"Mmm, it smells great in here." Parker said as he placed the bag carrying the dessert on the kitchen counter. "Is there anything I can do to help?"

"Would you pour the wine, please? I've got everything else under control," Kate said. "I think we're just about ready." Placing the food on the table, Kate watched as Parker poured the wine.

"Go ahead and sit down, I just have to get the bread and we're ready."

Kate and Parker made small talk as they ate, but eventually the talk turned to the murder investigation.

"How was the talk with the family?" Kate asked. Parker took a sip of wine before answering.

"Interesting, to say the least, it's looking like there may be no shortage of suspects. "

"Oh really? Why do you say that? Did she have that many enemies?"

"It's starting to sound that way. Or at least so far she doesn't seem to be the most likable person out there. I can't rule out any of her children, especially with her one son living right here. Or even his wife, for that matter. So far this is a disturbing case, and not just because she was killed. Getting to know the victim during an investigation, it gets so much more personal. But this time, getting to know Mrs. Phillips-Pierce, I guess I'm finding it just so sad. This is not turning out to be the normal family. I still have to talk to a couple of the siblings and her half-brother, but so far, it's been rather unsettling at the lack of feelings they seem to have had for her. Though from what they've been telling me, I guess I can't blame them. I guess that's what so sad about the whole thing. Imagine being murdered and your own kids don't really seem to care."

"God, that is sad. How do you keep these cases from taking a toll on you?" Kate asked as she poured more wine.

Parker gave a small smile, "I could almost ask the same of you, how you look at death every day, seeing what people can do to each other and themselves, and not let it bother you? Yes, I guess these cases do affect me, but you have to try and put it away and focus on getting the person responsible behind bars. Then at least there is justice for the victim and the people that cared about them. That's what it's all about, putting the killer behind bars and giving some sort of closure for the family."

"Well, for me, I guess it's a similar thing. Do the best I can do so you guys can find the bad guys. As far as the other cases, it makes me appreciate life that much more when I see people in my morgue that should never have been there, the ones that never took care of themselves. They made poor choices with their diet, lack of exercise, alcohol, or drugs. Sometimes it makes me mad, to look at how people can take something as precious as life and just throw it away. It just seems so senseless and tragic sometimes." Kate said sadly, shaking her head. "I guess all we can do is just enjoy life and do our best not to end up that way."

Parker agreed. "I guess that's something we have in

common," he said with a smile. "Now maybe we should talk about something lighter."

"You're right, I'm sorry. I told myself I wasn't going to talk shop tonight," Kate said. "So, how about those Hokies," she said laughing. Kate had gone to Virginia Tech and was naturally a huge fan. "I'll have to take you to a game sometime."

"I'd like that" Parker replied smiling. Kate has such an infectious laugh, he thought. And a beautiful smile. As Kate started clearing the table, Parker got up to assist.

"I'll get the dishes," he said as he moved to the sink and started washing the plates.

"Now that is something you don't see every day," Kate noted, "not that I'm complaining, mind you. Actually, I think a man that washes dishes is rather sexy."

Parker almost dropped the glass he was washing.

"I'm sorry, I'm making you blush," Kate said. "I didn't mean to make you uncomfortable."

"It's ok, I just never thought of it quite that way. I'm not sure I'll be able to look at a pan of dishwater the same way from now on." Parker and Kate both laughed.

As he put the last of the dishes in the rack to dry, Kate picked up their wine glasses and moved towards the living room.

"I think we'll be more comfortable in here," she said. Parker took his glass from Kate and followed into the living room, where they both settled on the couch.

"Ok, no more shop talk," Kate said smiling at Parker.

"Ok" Parker replied, smiling back. Putting his arm around Kate's shoulder he pulled her close. Lightly kissing her lips, he said "Maybe we shouldn't talk at all."

"Mmm," Kate replied, her lips still on Parker's, "I think you may be right," kissing him back.

8 CHAPTER EIGHT

Jonathan hung up the phone and sat staring at the kitchen wall. Stupid cop. Like some hick cop is going to solve his mother's murder, asking if he's been to Virginia lately or had any reason to kill his mother. Yeah, right, like I'm going to tell you anything you stupid cop. Listening to his kids arguing about their toys in the living room of the small apartment, memories came flooding back. He and Emily would fight over toys, their mother coming in and always siding with him. Poor Emily, being older than Jonathan, she always got blamed for anything. Jonathan knew he was his mother's favorite, and took full advantage. Sometimes he was amazed Emily talked to him at all considering how she was treated. He wondered how she was taking the news about their mother's death. No, not death, murder. Death would imply a heart attack or something. She was bludgeoned with a rock. Mom would have hated that, she was always so vain. Now here she was with her head bashed in. Jonathan thought about calling Graham, but decided against it. There was no love lost between the two, and now with Charlotte dead, there was no telling how Graham would react. Jonathan always felt that Graham only tolerated him because he didn't want to hear any crap from their mother. Well, time to head to Virginia and start playing the bereaved son. And find out about the will. This should be interesting. He wondered if the others knew about the inheritance, and how they would react. Bunch of assholes, treating him like a leper all these years, thinking when mom died they would inherit everything and he would go away. Well who has the last laugh now, Jonathan smiled. Yes indeed, this was going to be fun.

Then his thoughts returned to the phone call with the detective. *I need to get Kelly on the same page with our stories,* he thought. *That cop is going to call her, and it's probably best if we say the same thing and stick to it.* After all, despite appearances, he did have reason to kill his mother, fifteen million of them. Jonathan laughed out loud. Yes sir, fifteen million bucks was sounding really good right now. Now, he had to figure a way to keep the money out of Kelly's hands, and be sure she understood it was not going to be hers when he dies. God knows he doesn't want to end up with his head bashed in, and when money is involved, there is no telling what Kelly is capable of.

Jonathan got up and walked to the dimly lit bathroom, where Kelly was lounging in a bathtub full of rose scented water. Lit candles surrounded the tub, and music played softly in the background. Kelly lay back with her head on a pillow, eyes closed as she languished in the tub. Jonathan stared at her naked body, admiring her huge breasts, flat stomach and trim legs. He thought about the things she could do, and felt himself growing hard. Suddenly, Jonathan grabbed the top of Kelly's head and shoved her under the water, holding her for several seconds while she struggled and flailed at him before finally letting her up.

"What the hell are you doing?!" Kelly screamed at him. "Are

45

you trying to kill me?!"

Jonathan laughed and grabbed her head with one hand, while he unbuttoned his jeans with his other hand. "Not yet, though the thought has crossed my mind on occasion. Especially when I think of what you did. But for now, I have a better use for you and that magnificent body, and something else to occupy your mouth, so I don't have to listen to you. Plus, you can show me some of those tricks of the trade you learned during your so called movie career. And when I'm done with you, then we are going to talk about our alibis before that detective calls back. Remember, there is fifteen million dollars on the line, it will give you some incentive to think about while your lips are wrapped around my dick."

9 CHAPTER NINE

Miguel Aguerre and Eduardo Figueras rode back to the barn, discussing the days training. Professional polo players, they were getting ready for the upcoming season on Long Island.

"Looks like you have company," Eduardo noted. Miguel looked at where Eduardo indicated with a nod of his head, smiled.

"I'll catch up with you later for drinks at The Tavern," Eduardo laughed as he dismounted and handed his horse over to the groom standing by.

"Maybe amigo," Miguel replied. "Although I may be busy for a bit," he said with a grin as a groom took his horse away. He walked over to the fence where Charlotte stood waiting. Tall and good looking, with dark hair and eyes, the riding pants and tight white polo shirt showing off his toned body and dark skin, Miguel attracted attention from everyone around him. Particularly from the women, which Charlotte couldn't help noticing.

"Hello Miguel," she said as he stopped in front of her. Charlotte was dressed casually in a dark skirt and light blue blouse, her blond hair loosely pulled back.

"My dear Charlotte, to what do I owe this pleasure?" Miguel replied with a smile, showing impossibly white, straight teeth.

"We need to talk. Let's go somewhere quiet," Charlotte said.

"We can go to my apartment. I need to change out of these clothes and into something more appropriate for my lady." Miguel took Charlotte's hand and kissed it.

"I think it's better if we talk somewhere else. Get in the car, I'll drive."

Miguel raised an eyebrow but followed Charlotte to the car. "So, we are going where?" He asked as he got into the car.

"Bonny's," she replied, referring to a small restaurant a few miles away. "We should be able to talk in private there."

Pulling into the parking lot, Charlotte parked and waited while Miguel got out, walked around the car and opened the door for her. Without speaking, they walked into Bonny's and asked for a booth in the back corner, where it was darker and private.

After the waitress took their drink order, Miguel looked at Charlotte expectantly.

"Well?" he asked.

"I, uh," Charlotte started. "I, um, I'm pregnant," she finally said. Miguel stared at her, shock slowly turning to anger.

"How can that be?" he hissed at her, "You told me you were protected!"

"I was," she hissed back, "but these things happen!"

"And what are you going to do?" Miguel asked.

"What am I going to do? I have no idea what WE'RE going to do, that's why we're here!"

Miguel was stunned. The last thing he wanted right now was a wife and child, though, Charlotte's father was rich, and polo was very expensive. Perhaps something could be worked out. It wouldn't be the first time someone had to get married, and it didn't mean he had to change his lifestyle. He could still play polo, and have women on the side. Charlotte would just have to accept that.

"I guess we'll have to get married," Miguel finally said. After all, Charlotte was beautiful, rich, and fun in bed, although pretty spoiled and needy.

"Married? Don't be ridiculous. I can't marry you. People like me don't marry people like you. We'll have to think of something else."

Miguel's blood went cold. "You don't marry people like me? Does your father even know about us?"

"Of course not! You don't think I'd tell him I was having an affair with some polo player from Argentina, do you?" Charlotte snapped.

"In that case, I can find a doctor to take care of it. I am sure you will be able to pay for it." Miguel glared at Charlotte. How could he have been so stupid to get involved with her? Women were always coming on to him, and in these days of free love, he was never without a companion. Charlotte had always come off as a free spirit, despite her wealth. Someone who lived her life the way she wanted, rules be damned. Now, when she finds herself as a divorced woman with four kids, and pregnant by her lover, she's concerned with appearances.

"I am not going to some back street doctor for an abortion! I am

having this baby. I will do it without your help!" Charlotte got up and stormed out of the restaurant. Miguel jumped up and followed her out, but Charlotte was already in the car and putting it in reverse when he grabbed the passenger side door handle. Flooring the gas, Charlotte nearly ran over Miguel as he jumped back, screaming at her in Spanish. She put the car back in drive and tore out of the parking lot, leaving him standing there.

"Loco bitch!" he yelled at her rapidly receding taillights, before turning back to the restaurant to call for a ride back to the stables, not noticing the dark blue car that had followed them from the barn now turned and followed Charlotte's car as it sped down the road.

Thomas put down the phone. The private detective had finished giving his report. Thomas sighed, staring into space. What was he going to do with her? What was it with children these days? It was all those damn hippies, with their long hair, music, and civil rights. They were ruining the country. Sometimes he felt so old. Well, might as well call Victor and let him know. Thomas sighed again as he picked up the phone.

10 CHAPTER TEN

The wind was the first sign of the storm to come. There is stillness to the atmosphere that is felt just before the winds and rain of a hurricane. The wind was picking up now, and there was an uneasy feeling in the air. The hurricane was barreling up the coast, heading straight for Long Island, with landfall expected later that afternoon. Charlotte woke up to the sound of the wind, and an all too familiar pain. She cursed to herself as another contraction hit her. How the hell was she going explain this? She was sure she had hidden her pregnancy from everyone, adopting the hippie fashions of long, flowing skirts to hide her increasing belly. No matter, she was going to have to leave now, if she expected to make it off the island to have this baby out of state. It was imperative that no one find out. Charlotte intended to drive to Connecticut and leave the baby with a friend, until she could find a way to bring him into the family without anyone suspecting anything. Grabbing her suitcase, she threw her clothes in it, and grabbed her purse.

As she headed for the door, she encountered Emily, who was coming out of the bathroom.

"Mom, what's going on?" Noticing the suitcase she asked, "Are we leaving because of the hurricane? I haven't packed anything! Are we

leaving now?"

"No, you are staying here. I have to leave for a few days, a friend needs me."

"But Mom, there's a hurricane coming!" Emily cried. "How can you leave us? Who is going to stay with us?"

"You girls are big enough to stay by yourselves. Your brothers are in school and can't be here. The hurricane probably won't get here, so you'll be fine. Now go wake your sister so I can tell her what she needs to do and then I need to leave. "

"Mom, I'm scared, can't you stay with us, please?" Begged Emily as the rain started, thunder rumbling in the distance as flashes of lighting lit the sky.

"Emily, stop it! I've already told you, I need to leave. Now grow up and stop acting like a baby. You're eight years old now, there is no reason you can't be alone with your sister. Ellen! Where are you? I need to talk to you, now!"

Ellen came out of her bedroom, rubbing her eyes.

"What's going on? Is it about the hurricane?"

"I need to leave for a few days, and you need to take care of Emily while I'm gone. There is plenty of food here, and you can call the neighbors if you need anything. I'll be back in a few days."

"What? What about the hurricane? You're leaving us alone now?!" Ellen was shocked. At ten she was used to her mother's crazy behavior, but this was something else. There was a hurricane heading right towards them, and she was leaving them alone?

"I told you it will be fine. There is always a chance it won't hit. There is enough food that you can eat if the power goes out, and you know how to call the power company to report it. If you need anything else, you can ask Mrs. Devoe next door. I'm sure she will help you. Now, I want you to be my big girls, and I'll be back in a few days." *Before the girls could protest any further, Charlotte picked up her suitcase, walked out the door, getting into the brand new Ford Country Squire station wagon, and drove down the driveway. Ellen stared after her, astonished.*

"I can't believe she just did that!" she said.

"Ellen, I'm so scared, what if the hurricane comes? What will we do?" Emily cried.

"We'll be ok, honey," Ellen hugged her little sister. "Look, we have Lady. She'll protect us, just like Lassie," she said as Lady came over and started licking the tears from Emily's face. Emily wrapped her arms around Lady's neck, burying her face in her soft fur.

"You'll keep us safe, won't your girl, just like Lassie?" she sobbed. Lady whined softly and slowly wagged her tail, not understanding what her mistress was upset about, but doing what she could to try and make Emily feel better.

"Maybe we should call Jake and Graham." Emily said.

Ellen thought a moment, and then sighed. "I don't think so, not yet anyway. You know how Jake gets, there is no telling what he would do." Then noticing the look on Emily's face, she added, "Don't worry, we can call if we need to, but we're going to be ok. Now, I guess we should go ahead and make breakfast, and get some water set aside in case the power goes out. Come on, it'll be like an adventure, can you imagine how jealous the boys will be when they find out we got to be by ourselves in a hurricane?" Ellen faked a smile for her sister's benefit. Taking Emily's hand, she led her into the kitchen to start making breakfast.

The rain was really coming down as Charlotte drove along the expressway, fighting to control the car as the wind buffeted the car. The wipers were having a harder time keeping the windshield clear as she drove along. Driving over the bridge was scary, as the wind was much worse. The contractions were still far enough apart that she felt she would be able to get to the hospital in time, as long as she didn't encounter any problems on the road. One thing about the hurricane, at least there weren't as many people on the road. "I just hope none of the roads are blocked," she thought as another contraction hit her.

Ellen and Emily both jumped when the lights blipped out. The wind was really howling, whipping the rain around the house. The thunder and lightning was almost instantaneous now. The wind and rain were so loud it almost drowned out the sound.

"Maybe we could call Dad," Emily looked hopefully at Ellen.

"Dad's in Texas on business, remember?" Ellen replied. "Look, we'll be ok. We can always camp out in the basement until it's over. Let's get some games and the flashlights. We'll bring the brownies Mom made last night and have a party. It will be fun, I promise." Emily shivered as the lights flickered and then went out, and then agreed.

"Ok, let's go. Don't forget Lady," she said.

"Of course we can't forget Lady," Ellen replied as she grabbed the brownies and some drinks. "And let's not forget pillows and blankets and candles, too." Ellen wished she felt as confident as she was pretending to be. Damn Mom for leaving them alone like this. What if a tree falls on the house? How could she just leave like that? What friend could be more important that her own children? Ellen wanted to cry, but knew Emily was having a hard enough time without her breaking down,

too. *Maybe she should call Jake. It would serve Mom right if Jake got mad and yelled at her. At fourteen, Jake was over six feet tall, and solid muscle from playing football. Ellen was a bit intimidated by her older brother, he was quick to blow up and have a temper tantrum. Not like Graham,* she thought. *Graham was quiet and logical, always thinking of solutions to problems first, before reacting. He would know what to do. Though he had a temper, too, he was slower to anger, and tended to keep his feelings to himself. Ellen tended to be something of a dreamer, preferring to stay in her room and read or draw, listening to her albums and blocking out the real world. Emily was the tomboy of the family. Always playing outside, finding injured animals, snakes or birds, and bringing them home to nurse back to health. Emily also adored her older sister, and tried to emulate her, doing her own drawings, though hers tended to be of animals, while Ellen's were usually flowers and landscapes.*

Ellen and Emily lit the candles and headed down to the safety of the basement, a large finished room with couches, and a pool table in the middle of the room. Off to one side was the laundry area, where the washer and dryer were located, along with a table to fold clothes and an ironing board. The girls set up the pillows and blankets on the floor, along with the food, drinks and board games. At least in the basement the storm wasn't as loud and they tried to pretend it was just a bad thunderstorm.

"Well, this isn't so bad," Ellen said as they opened one of the games.

"Yeah, it's not as scary down here." Emily responded. "I guess we can do this, though I'm still mad at Mom for leaving us alone like this. Why does she always do this to us?"

"I don't know, I guess her friend really needed her more than we do. I just hope she isn't gone that long; Mrs. Devoe will have a fit. I bet

Mom didn't even tell her she was leaving us alone again. Remember that time Mrs. Devoe tried to tell Mom she shouldn't leave us alone and Mom started screaming at her to mind her own business?"

"Yeah, she sure was mad that day."

"Poor Mrs. Devoe, she was only trying to help and Mom starts cursing at her. I thought Mrs. Devoe was going to call the cops on her."

The hurricane was picking up, the sounds of the howling winds and rain penetrated to the basement. Suddenly a loud crash startled both girls, causing them both to jump. Lady whined and stood by the girls, putting her nose in Ellen's hand as the lights flickered, but stayed on.

"What was that?" cried Emily.

"I think it was a tree, I sure hope that didn't hit the house!" Ellen hugged her little sister. "We'll just stay here, I'm not going upstairs until this is over, then we can see what happened. Besides, we have Lady to protect us."

"Ok" said Emily, "I sure wish Graham or Jake were here. Or Dad."

"I know,me to," Ellen replied, "me too."

Charlotte barely held back a scream as she gave one last push. "It's a boy!" the doctor exclaimed as he held up the newborn baby. Quickly the nurses took the baby and cleaned him up, before handing him to Charlotte.

"Congratulations, here you go," the nurse said as she handed the baby to Charlotte. Looking at her new son for the first time, Charlotte saw how much he looked like his father, olive skin, a head full of jet black hair. And what a set of lungs, she thought as the baby started squalling.

"Shhh," she said as she held him close, giving him a little kiss. "There is no need to cry, my beautiful son; Mama's going to take good care of you. You will have a wonderful life, don't you worry."

11 CHAPTER ELEVEN

Parker hung up the phone and stared at the wall facing his desk. This case was not going to be easy. Graham was right; there was no lack of potential suspects in this case, starting with the family. Parker sighed and leaned back in his chair. The funeral was the day after tomorrow. It would give him an opportunity to see who showed up, and get a better feel for the family dynamics. From what he learned so far, there was a lot of tension and bad feelings in the family, all due to Charlotte and how she treated her children and those around her. She definitely was an interesting character, even if not a particularly likable one. Parker's musings were interrupted by his cell phone. Glancing at the number, he groaned. Karen, what did she want?

"Hello."

"Hi. I just called to see how you were doing. I heard you got that murder on the trail."

"I'm doing fine," Parker replied, trying to keep his voice even.

"Oh. Ok. If you need to talk about it, we can have a drink

sometime, "Karen said.

"I'm fine," Parker repeated, "That won't be necessary. Look Karen, I'm really busy right now with this case. I've got to go."

"Too busy for me you mean. You're not too busy for Kate Spade." Karen replied icily.

"That's enough. You and I are no longer dating, so my personal life is no longer any of your business."

"Yes, I know, I remember. You don't have to be an ass about it. I was just trying to be polite. Screw you Parker." Karen slammed down the phone.

Parker shook his head. What did he ever see in her to begin with? Why couldn't she just accept it was over, and move on? What a pain in the ass. Just then his phone rang again. Parker answered without looking.

"What," he snapped.

"Bad time?" Kate's velvety smooth voice was in his ear.

"Oh sorry Kate, I didn't see it was you. I thought it was Karen again. She just called, and put me in a bad mood, I guess."

"I see. Am I interrupting anything? I was going to suggest getting together for a drink, but if you have plans, we can do it another time."

"No, you're not interrupting anything and a drink sounds wonderful. Do you want me to pick you up? I have a few things to settle here, after that I can stop by your place, say half an hour?"

"That will work just fine. I'm on my way home. I'll see you in a bit." Kate smiled as she hung up, humming along with the radio as she drove. It's too bad Karen couldn't accept that Parker had moved on. Kate hoped Karen wasn't going to be an ongoing problem, Parker was just too nice to let go because he has a loony ex. She didn't know why Karen resented her so much. She didn't have anything to do with the breakup. That had been months before she and Parker started dating. Oh well, Karen will just have to get over it.

Later, Parker and Kate walked into the restaurant and asked for a booth at the back, where it was more private. Over drinks and appetizers, they discussed the case.

"How is the case going, any progress?" Kate asked.

"This case is turning into a nightmare." Parker said. "This woman was something else. I've talked to all her family, and it's been quite an eye opener. I think you and I are about the only ones so far that I've crossed off the suspect list."

"Oh my, she can't be that bad, seriously?" Kate asked.

"You would not believe, and I'm just cracking the surface. I can't wait to see what, if anything, happens at the funeral. It will be interesting to see who shows up, and what they have to say. I'm betting it will be pretty full, just with all the publicity the murder has been getting."

"Hmm, I was thinking of showing up myself, after doing the post on her, I feel like I've got my own connection to her. I hope I don't see another one like that any time soon. No matter how she was in life, she didn't deserve to die like that. It never fails to amaze me the horrible things people can do to each other."

"I know what you mean. If people could see what goes on in other folk's homes, they wouldn't believe it. You would be amazed at what goes on, and who is doing it. I've seen husbands beat the hell out of their wives in very expensive homes, with fancy cars parked in the driveway. Or those are the ones with the alcohol or drug problems. Everyone thinks it's the poor people doing it, but I've seen just as much inhumanity to man in rich people's homes, as in the poor."

"That's so true. What people also don't realize is that no matter who you are, or how rich or poor, eventually you will end up on my table." Kate replied. "So in the end, does it matter? Isn't better to try and live a good life and be a good person?"

"If everyone did that, I'd be out of a job," laughed Parker.

"Well, it's a thought. Besides, then you could join your buddy Squirrel chasing dead people." Kate was laughing now, too. "I can see you now, trying to interview a ghost."

Parker smiled at the thought. "Yeah, I can just see it now. You know, you really do need to meet Squirrel, he's a good dude. Maybe once this case is over we can get together with him and his wife. "

"That would be nice, I'd like that. I'd love to meet him. Anyone that goes from being a SWAT team member to paranormal investigator has to be one interesting guy. Maybe you should have him ask Charlotte who killed her, and then you could wrap this one up."

"If only it were that easy, trust me, I already tried that," Parker replied laughing. "I'm glad you called, this has been a nice break, I really needed it, especially today."

"Me too, this has been nice. I'm glad you agreed to come out tonight." Kate smiled over her glass of wine.

Parker smiled back. "Next I'm going to have to get you out mountain biking with me, you would really enjoy it."

"I'm not so sure about that," laughed Kate, "I haven't been on a bike since I was a kid. I don't know if I can handle that."

"You'll be fine, as they say, it's just like riding a bike," Parker smiled. "It's a really great way to unwind. It's just you and the bike, rolling through the woods, admiring the flora and fauna, seeing the wildlife up close."

"It sounds lovely. Ok, we'll have to give it a try."

Parker smiled, "Great, It's a date."

Karen sat in her car across from the restaurant. *That bastard! Too busy for drinks, my ass! What does he call what he's doing now? Having drinks with Kate. How dare he to lie to me,* she thought. Blinking back tears; Karen started the car, and with a squeal of rubber, tore out of the parking spot and sped down the road.

Karen stopped at a local bar frequented by other medics. Stomping through the door, she noticed several of her friends at a table. As she approached, Mike, a good looking medic she often worked with, held out a chair for her. He was dressed in his signature outfit of jeans, Western style shirt, and cowboy boots.

"Thanks," she said as she sat down.

"What are you drinking?" Mike asked.

"I'll have a beer, thanks," she replied.

Mike flagged down the waitress and gave her the order.

"What's got you all pissed off?" he asked.

"Parker, what else?" she answered.

"I thought you two were done," Mike said, "What did he do?"

"We are. I just need to move on," Karen took a swallow of her beer. "He's such an ass."

"Well," Mike smiled as he leaned in closer, "if you are serious about moving on, I just may know someone willing to help you forget about him."

Karen studied his face for a moment, and then smiled suggestively, "I'll bet you do. So tell me, how are you going to make me forget?"

"Why don't you finish that beer, and come with me? I have some really good ideas." Mike placed his hand lightly on the back of her neck, leaned closer and kissed her on the lips.

Finishing her beer, Karen smiled back, "Lead the way, cowboy."

Graham and Stella pulled up to the church. Even though the memorial service wasn't due to start for another hour, the parking lot was filling up fast.

"You OK?" Stella asked Graham.

"Yeah. Let's get this over with. I hate this stuff."

As they got out of the car, someone called out to him. Turning, he saw his brother Jake coming towards him, followed by Jake's wife, Gina.

"Hey man," Jake said as he came up and gave Graham a quick hug, "good to see you. Can you believe all this?"

"Good to see you, too," Graham replied. "I still can't get my head around it. I always figured it would happen, but that doesn't make it any easier to deal with. What a mess."

"What's the latest? Have they got any suspects yet?"

"You mean besides all of us? Not that I'm aware of. I'm sure Detective Williams will be here today, but the last time I talked to him, no one had been ruled out as a suspect. "

The four of them walked into the church, Stella and Gina walked together, as their husbands talked.

"This has just been a nightmare," Stella told Gina. "It's scary to think someone murdered Charlotte. You wonder, was this a random act, or was she the intended victim? What if they are targeting the family? You never know with these things."

"I know, it must really be hard for you guys living here. At least there is some distance with us. Jake is taking it pretty hard. He's been snapping at any little thing, yelling at me or the kids all the time, not sleeping. I tried to tell him maybe he needs to talk to someone, and he went into a rage, telling me he knows what he's doing and doesn't need some shrink."

"Jeez, I'm sorry. I don't know what to say. I know Jake tends to be a bit volatile, I don't know how you deal with it. I can tell Graham is upset, but he tends to be the opposite. He holds everything in, and then goes off for some stupid reason. It's not like when Victor died, at least he had time to talk to him and resolve old issues. This was so sudden and unexpected."

"I know. I miss Victor, he was a bit of a stiff, that old hard ass British attitude, but he treated everyone fairly. Not like Charlotte with her favorite son." Gina rolled her eyes. "I guess he will be here today, playing the bereaved son for all it's worth."

"I'm sure. You know he'll be right up front and center stage, as usual. I can hardly wait."

Stella and Gina were joined by Ellen and Emily.

After everyone hugged each other and said their condolences, they watched as the room began to fill up. Stella was the first to notice the couple coming in the door.

"Speak of the devil, here comes the little prince." She said as Jonathan and his wife came towards them. "Hang onto your husbands, Kelly is here," Stella continued as they approached. Jonathan was good looking, medium height and build, with dark hair and eyes, olive skin reflecting his Spanish heritage.

Kelly was also very attractive. The same height as her husband, her tailored suit showed off her trim body and large breasts. Thick straight brown hair fell to her shoulders, brown eyes in an aristocratic face, with high cheekbones and straight, upturned nose.

"Nice nose job," Gina noted.

"The better to look down on her subjects, I guess," Stella added.

"It looks like she's bought some new boobs, too."

"Gina and Stella, stop it!" Ellen scolded, "She's not that bad."

"Oh come on, Ellen, stop being such a Pollyanna. I'll bet she has her next Mercedes all picked out already. And, she's thanking her lucky stars Jonathan changed his mind about the divorce, or she would have to find her next rich husband," Gina snapped.

"Ok, that's enough" Ellen said. "Let's try to remember why we're here. This is our mother who's dead."

"You're right, but I still can't stand that woman, and I don't trust her." Gina replied.

"That makes two of us," Stella added, "But Ellen is right, let's remember, she and Emily did lose their mom. I'm sorry Ellen. Besides, I see Kelly heading for Jake and Graham. Come on Gina, let's go remind her they are married."

"I can't believe them," Ellen said to Emily.

"Cut them some slack, they're right about Kelly, she's an obvious gold digger. Don't forget, she was married when she met Jonathan, and dumped her husband when she realized Jonathan had more money, and stood to gain more when Mom died. "

"Ok, you're right. I'm just so upset about all this. I never imagined this happening to Mom."

"Well, that puts you in the minority then. Who do you suppose killed her? I wonder if the ax murderer got out. I know Mom was getting mail and calls from him, saying he was going to be paroled soon and was planning on coming and living with her, since she had been writing him all those years."

"I don't know. She told me the same thing. She was pretty

freaked out that he wanted to come live with her. That was typical, though, send him all that money while he's in prison, tell him how wonderful he is, and never stop to think he might get out. Or how betrayed he will feel if she doesn't go to the parole board and make a case for him getting out. Did you know about that?" Ellen asked Emily.

"I heard something about it. He wanted her to go to the parole hearing, and she made some excuse. I heard he was pretty upset about it. Maybe he got out and killed her, or had someone else do it."

"Well, you can tell that to the detective, there he is," Ellen said, pointing him out.

Parked approached the sisters.

"I just want to say again how sorry I am. I also want to let you know, I'm not going to stop until I find out who did this to your mother."

"Thank you detective," Ellen said. "We were just talking about who it could be, and had some more information about Kevin Whitman you may not have been aware of." Ellen and Emily quickly filled in the details they had been discussing.

"That's good information, thank you," Parker said. "Let me know if you can think of anything else. Any little detail helps. You never know what will be the break we need to solve this."

"We will Detective. Now if you'll excuse us, we need to go be with the rest of the family. The service should be starting soon."

Kate joined Parker as he watched Emily and Ellen walk off.

"Nice looking family," she said. "Did you see the youngest son and his wife? He definitely does not have the same father as the others, and the wife looks like a piece of work. Class A snob, if you ask me."

"Are you sure you don't want to be a detective? Your powers of observation are amazing."

"Being an ME is like being a detective, remember. It's all in the details and putting the story together," Kate smiled at Parker.

"Good point." Parker smiled back. "Shall we go take our seats?" he said as he took Kate's elbow and guided her to their seats.

Kelly glanced around as she and Jonathan sat down. The coolness coming from Stella and Gina as they greeted her and Jonathan was unmistakable. They had never liked or accepted her as part of the family. Well, she wouldn't have to deal with them much longer, Thank God. She was tired of trying to pretend she cared about any of these people. Once the will was settled, she and Jonathan would have the money Charlotte promised them, and they would never have to deal with any of these assholes again. That would teach them. She couldn't wait to see the looks on their faces when they find out Charlotte left everything to Jonathan. Kelly smiled at the thought. Soon it would be all over.

Later, after the service, Parker and Kate followed the family to the grave site, though they hung back to observe. They noticed how Jonathan and Kelly stood apart from the other siblings.

"Interesting, don't you think?" Parker asked Kate.

"Yes, it is. It doesn't seem like he's very well-liked by the

68

others, does it?" Kate answered.

"No, it sure doesn't."

After the graveside service, the family walked back to their cars. They were all going back to Graham and Stella's house.

"All right, everyone follow us," Graham said as he and Stella got into their car.

"OK, lead the way," Emily replied.

At the house, everyone mingled around, getting caught up, talking about the service, but mostly, the murder.

Jake was talking to Ellen. "Where is Daniel?" he asked, referring to Ellen's current husband.

"He couldn't make it, he had a job to do that he couldn't reschedule." Daniel was a self-employed contractor.

"Of course he couldn't," Jake responded.

"Don't start, "Ellen snapped, "Daniel works very hard, and the jobs aren't out there like they used to be. We need every one he can find. I'm tired of everyone getting on his case. Just because he doesn't drop everything to come to family get- togethers doesn't mean he doesn't care."

"Ok, I'm sorry. I wasn't picking on the guy," Jake said. "It's just he never seems to be around for these things. Makes us think he doesn't like us or something. Anyway, I thought you two were on the outs."

"Not anymore. We were separated, but we're back together now."

Just then Emily came up. "That was a nice service, Mom would have liked it."

"Yes she would have," Ellen responded, her eyes tearing up.

"So what happens now?" Emily asked.

"I guess we find out about the will, put the house up for sale and go home." Jake replied.

"Is that all you care about? The money?" Ellen asked.

"It doesn't matter to me. I heard the bitch left everything to Jonathan, though I plan on contesting it. It shouldn't be too hard to show she was nuts and he was taking advantage of her. Besides, what has she ever done for me? She was never there when I needed her. It was all about Charlotte and then Jonathan. That's all that mattered to her. At least now that she's dead, I won't have to listen to it anymore."

Ellen appeared shocked at Jake's outburst. How could he be so callous? Then she thought about what he said about the will, was it true? Emily beat her to asking the question.

"Where did you hear that she left everything to Jonathan? That's not what she used to tell me, she said she was taking care of all of us. That can't be true."

"It's true. Just ask Graham, he's the one that told me. He saw a copy of it, pissed him off to no end, too. "

Emily called Graham over to their group. "Jake says Mom left everything to Jonathan, that can't be," she said.

"Yes, she did. I saw the will. None of her four original

children get a dime. Jonathan gets everything because he never had a father."

"What? How can she say that? He has a father. She just didn't have the guts to marry the guy. What she means is, he didn't have a rich father. She thinks Dad left us so much money, but he didn't have nearly what she has. Who is she kidding?" Emily appeared pissed now, too. Ellen was looking pale. It was no secret she and Daniel were struggling financially. Daniel having started a business with Ellen's savings that failed, leaving them in bad financial straits. It was also rumored Daniel had a drinking problem, adding to the stress. Jake was also in a bind financially, having re-mortgaged his house several times to pay for his lavish lifestyle, always expecting to inherit from his parents and be able to live the life he became accustomed to.

"No wonder Kelly looks so smug. I bet she knows damn well who gets the money. Well, I'm not giving up without a fight. That's our inheritance. After all we went through growing up, and it's the least we deserve," Emily said.

"Well, Mom did dote on Kelly, the way Kelly was always sucking up to her," Graham said. "I'll bet if Mom knew about what Kelly had done, she wouldn't be so enamored of her. It's only because she's married to Jonathan. How convenient for Kelly they didn't get divorced yet."

"I don't trust either one of them," Stella said as she walked up. "It wouldn't surprise me if Kelly was blackmailing Jonathan over something. I can't believe he took her back after that. God knows what either of them is up to."

"Isn't that the truth," Gina agreed. "Well, we have to get

back to the motel. It's been a long day. We'll meet you for breakfast tomorrow, if you feel like coming into town."

"Sure, that sounds good. I guess we'll have to ask Jonathan and Kelly if they care to join us. If we're lucky, they will say no." Graham said, as he walked over to talk to Jonathan.

"Well, goodbye, we'll see you tomorrow," Jake said as he and got ready to go. "Ellen, are you and Emily coming, too?"

"Yeah, hang on. We'll go ahead of you since we know the way back to town. You can follow us."

"We're coming, too," said Jonathan. "We'll follow all of you guys."

Stella watched as they all drove down the driveway. Thank God they were gone. Maybe now she and Graham could get some peace. It was always so stressful having his siblings around.

"Hey," she called to Graham. "I think we need to hop on the bikes and hit the trails. I know I need to burn off some stress."

"Good idea, though we will have to ride here, I don't want to drive into town again today."

"That's fine, let's get changed and go."

* * *

"Hey Squirrel," Parker said into the phone.

"Howdy. What's going on? Did you find the killer yet?"

"Not yet, I was just at the funeral. That was interesting. There is a lot of tension and jealousies in that family. Any one of them could have a reason to kill her, and that's just the family. I've talked to other people who knew her and I tell you, it would be easier to eliminate those that didn't have a reason to kill her and go from there. I'm beginning to think I should give up this detective business and join you looking for ghosts."

Squirrel laughed. "I'm not so sure you want to do that. I have a case I just got involving two middle aged ladies that got more than they bargained for playing with an Ouija board. Whatever happened to playing Canasta or Bridge?"

Parker laughed back. "You're kidding, right?"

"Nope, I'm serious. Seems they have a weekly séance, put on a Black Sabbath record, some candles, and break out the Ouija board. "

"That's too funny, just trying to picture it. Do they have cats, too?"

"Of course, a Siamese named Witchy Poo. "

Parker nearly choked on his coffee. "Witchy Poo? Seriously man, you're making this up, aren't you?"

"I'm telling you, I can't make this stuff up. But get this, this is the best part. Guess who they're trying to contact?"

"I'm afraid to ask," Parker responded laughing.

"They are contacting one woman's dead husband. It seems he was really paranoid about the government trying to get his money, so he refused to keep it in a bank. They're trying to contact him to find out where the money is."

"Oh my God, that is too funny. You're right, you can't make this stuff up." Parker said as he wiped tears from his eyes.

"Well, did I ever tell you about the woman that insisted her house was haunted because her dog kept barking at the wall? "

"No, but this should be good." Parker replied.

"Yeah, she has a miniature Schnauzer. The dog kept going to the wall, scratching and barking. She insisted it was something paranormal. I get there and sure enough, the dog is hanging out being a dog, and then goes nuts, charging the wall, barking nonstop. We do some investigating around the house, and find a hole in a wall in the attic above where the dog is going nuts. Turns out she had raccoons in her wall."

"Ok, stop, I can't take anymore," Parker said laughing. "That is just nuts. I don't know how you do it. I think I'll stick with the job I have, thanks."

"Well, if you change your mind, just give me a call. It might be a good break for you. In the meantime, I have to go help these ladies get whatever they let loose back where it belongs. I'll talk to you later."

"Ok, man, have fun. I'll catch up with you later. Tell those ghosts to get on back where they belong."

"You got it. Have a good one," Squirrel said as he hung up the phone.

Jonathan took another sip from his drink. He sat on the balcony of the hotel, staring out at the mountains, brooding.

"Hey honey," Kelly said as she joined him on the balcony. "What a day. I'm glad that's over with. Did you see the way your sisters and Stella treated me? Who do they think they are? Even your brothers hardly talked to me. It's like I wasn't even there."

"Can you blame them? Let's see, you ran off with our daughter to go be an "actress" for some asshole who makes porn movies because you think he is richer than I am. Not to mention you starring in those movies, as if exposing Morgan to that trashy lifestyle wasn't bad enough. Then you come crawling back to me after social services comes looking for you to take Morgan away. What did you think, my family would take you back with open arms? Be serious."

"Are you going to throw that in my face forever? Morgan wasn't hurt. No one touched her despite what you think. And besides, I don't hear you complaining about my talents, especially when you are watching my movies."

"I'm just telling you why my family doesn't want to deal with you. I'm done talking about this crap. I want to get this over with and go back to living my life without having to listen to my mother tell me what to do and what to think every second of every day."

"Well, soon we won't have to deal with them, if you don't want to. Once the will is read and the estate settled, we are done with them," Kelly ran her fingers slowly down Jonathan's arm, and then leaned over to kiss him on the cheek. "How are you doing, baby? I know this has been hard on you."

Jonathan leaned back in his chair. "I'm ok. It really hasn't sunk in yet that she's gone. It's going to be weird without her constant phone calls and visits. I guess at least we don't have to worry about her coming to stay with us anymore. I know how stressful that was for you. It wasn't like she was easy to deal with."

Kelly stroked Jonathan's cheek. "No, she wasn't. But she could be ok at times. As long as the checks kept coming, she was bearable," Kelly smiled sweetly at Jonathan, then slowly and gently lowered herself onto his lap, facing him.

"You're right about that, the money did make it bearable," Jonathan smiled as he started undoing the buttons on Kelly's blouse. "Let's see what else we can do to get our minds of this whole mess," he said as he removed her blouse and unhooked her bra. Kelly quickly unbuttoning his shirt as she leaned forward and locked her mouth on his, tongues playing against each other. Jonathan shoved Kelly's skirt above her hips; barely registering she wasn't wearing underwear, as she freed his penis from his pants.

"Hurry," she moaned into his mouth as he lowered her onto him, their hips moving in a rhythm that got progressively faster until Kelly arched her back and screamed in pleasure, Jonathan climaxing moments later. Kelly leaned forward and gently kissed him on the lips. "Maybe we should move to the bed and do this again, if you're up for it, that is," she giggled.

"Give me a minute and you're on," Jonathan replied as he stood up, and in one fluid motion picked up Kelly and carried her to the bed where they both collapsed. "Now, where were we?" he said as he lowered his mouth to hers.

Gina handed Jake a glass of wine, as she sat next to him on the hotel bed. "I can't believe what a bitch Kelly is. Did you see the way she and Jonathan walked in and acted like they were royalty? Who are they kidding? They didn't give a crap about your mother, all she was to them was a checkbook."

"Yeah, they are so freaking arrogant. I'm glad I don't have to look at their pompous faces much longer. I hope Mom is satisfied she raised such a jerk. What a couple of phonies. How about the way Jonathan got all choked up during the service and Kelly pretended to console him. I haven't seen such bad acting since O.J. tried on the damn glove," Jake raged.

"I know it was pretty pathetic. I can't believe they thought anyone would fall for that crap," Gina replied.

"They just piss me off so much. I can't stand those arrogant jerks. Too bad Mom had to bring that brat home. She's ruined everyone's lives because of him."

"Ok Jake, remember your blood pressure, I don't want anything happening to you because you're upset."

"I'm fine. I'm not going to keel over. I wouldn't give those assholes the satisfaction," Jake said angrily. Finishing his glass of wine in one final gulp, Jake got up. "I've got to make a couple of calls, and then I'm going to bed."

"Ok," Gina responded," I'm going to try and get some sleep, too. It's been a long day. Don't stay up too late, you're going to need your energy for tomorrow."

12 CHAPTER TWELVE

Charlotte walked in the house carrying a small child in her arms. "Ellen, Emily! Come here, I want you to meet someone."

The girls came down from their rooms and stood before their mother.

"Girls, I want you to meet your new brother, Jonathan," Charlotte said as she set the child down.

"What? What do you mean brother?" Ellen asked. "We already have brothers. You didn't ask us if we wanted another one."

"Ellen!" snapped Charlotte, "I've adopted Jonathan. He is now a part of the family, and you will treat him like you do Graham and Jake. Be nice to him, he doesn't have a father and deserves a family, too."

"But Mom, couldn't we have a sister instead?" Emily implored.

"No! You have a new brother, so get used to it. I expect you to be nice and get along. Do you hear me?" Charlotte put her hand on Jonathan's back. "Now, I also expect you to take good care of him, so you watch Jonathan while I make something for dinner."

The girls watched their mother walk into the kitchen, then turned to stare at Jonathan, who hadn't moved since Charlotte put him down. Ellen looked at the small child, with his dark hair, large brown eyes and smooth olive skin and sighed. "Come on, we might as well show you around," she said as she picked him up and headed towards the den. "Just wait until Jake and Graham hear this."

Jake inhaled on the joint he was holding as he watched Graham approach. Jake was in a new hiding spot he discovered in the woods that surrounded the football field of the school. "He looks ready to kill," he thought as he let the smoke fill his lungs before slowly exhaling. " I wonder what the problem is this time."

"Hey little brother, what's got you so pissed off?" Jake said as Graham stopped and stood in front of him.

"I've been looking all over the school for you. I should have known you'd be out here getting high."

"Yeah, well, you should give it a try before you condemn me for it. It's the only thing that makes being here bearable. So what's going on?"

Graham shook his head as he replied, "I just heard from the girls. It seems we have a new brother."

Jake was in the middle of inhaling again when he started coughing.

"What? What the hell are you talking about?"

"It appears dear old Mom has adopted some little kid. His name is Jonathan. The girls were pretty upset, even more so when Mom jumped on them when they said they didn't need another brother."

Jake had to laugh at that. "Man, I would have liked to have seen that. You know how she is when you question anything she does. I'm sure she was pretty pissed off. I can't believe she adopted some kid, what is that all about?"

"Hell if I know. I can't believe it. She doesn't even care about us, why would she want another kid?"

Jake inhaled again on the joint before responding. "Maybe we're getting too old for her to bully around and she needs someone who won't question her. Some little kid who will adore her and believe her lies when she says she cares. Wonder if Dad knows."

Graham sighed. "Ellen didn't say and she was afraid to ask Mom, you know how she gets. I feel sorry for the girls, it sounds like they are expected to take care of him."

"Yeah, she'll use them as built in babysitters. Maybe it's not so bad being here. At least we don't have to deal with that crap."

"I guess." Graham sighed again before nodding at the joint in his brother's hand. "Let me give it a try, I think I need it." Jake laughed as he handed over the joint.

"Way to go little brother, way to go."

Ellen opened the door to the basement. "Lady! Come on girl, where are you?" she called. Getting no response she closed the door and went to the kitchen where Charlotte was unloading groceries.

"Mom, I can't find Lady anywhere. Have you seen her?" Ellen looked worriedly at her mother.

"Lady isn't here anymore." Charlotte replied not looking at her daughter. "Now why don't you go check on Jonathan?"

"What do you mean she's not here anymore? Where is she? What's happened to Lady?"

"Lady had to be put to sleep. Now stop asking about her and go find your brother."

Ellen stared horrified for a moment before bursting into tears. "What? Why did you do it? She wasn't sick!"

Charlotte turned to her daughter. "Ellen stop it. She was just a dog. Jonathan is allergic to dogs, so she had to be put to sleep. Now, I don't want to hear any more about it. Go find your brother and make sure he's ok."

"She wasn't just a dog, she was my best friend! How could you do that? You didn't even ask me, you just killed her!" Ellen was sobbing hysterically.

"I said enough! You will get over it. Jonathan was having too many problems breathing with her around, so she had to go. Now I don't want to hear another word on the subject." Charlotte glared at her young daughter.

"I hate you, I hate you, I hate you!" Ellen screamed at her mother. "I'll never get over it, I loved Lady and she loved me! All you care about is Jonathan, you don't care about us! I want to go live with Dad! I don't want to live here anymore!" Ellen turned and ran, sobbing, out of the room.

"Ellen! I will not have you talking that way to me!" Charlotte yelled.

"I hate you!" Ellen screamed before slamming her bedroom door shut.

Charlotte threw down the bread she was holding. "God damn kids!"

"What's going on?" Emily asked as she came into the room. "Mom?"

"Your sister is behaving like a spoiled brat is what is going on. She's upset because Jonathan is allergic to dogs and Lady had to be put to sleep."

Emily stared at her mother. "No! Not Lady!"

"Don't you start with me, either. I've had enough for one day."

"But Mom, Lady was family! How could you?" Emily wailed.

"I said, I'm not going to discuss it. Now go find your brother, I have things to do."

"He's not my brother! I don't want him, I want Lady! Why didn't you get rid of him and keep Lady? She was our family!" Emily screamed at her mother.

Charlotte turned and slapped Emily across the face. "Don't you dare say that again!" she raged "Jonathan is your brother whether you like it or not. I will NOT have you talk to me like that! Now go to your room and stay there until I say you can come out!"

Emily glared at her mother through her tears, then turned and ran to the room she shared with her sister, slamming the door behind her.

Charlotte stared for a moment, shaking, listening to the sobbing of the girls. "Damn you Lady," she said blinking back the tears in her eyes. "Damn you."

13 CHAPTER THIRTEEN

Kenny was at his computer when Parker entered the station house.

"Hey Parker, check this out." Kenny called when Parker approached.

"What is it?" Parker asked as he stopped at Kenny's desk, peering at the computer screen.

"Well, I was doing a search on your murder victim. Get this. She was from an incredibly wealthy family. See, that's the thing about being that rich, people love to talk and read about you. Therefore, any little scandal is out there on the web. As a teenager, there was some sort of scandal, and she was sent to a really ritzy private school in Switzerland. It was while she was attending college there that she met her first husband."

"First husband, I didn't realize she had been married before."

"Yeah, well, it gets better. They got married after she graduated. He of course was also super rich. They lived all over Europe, traveled everywhere, led the lifestyle of the super-rich, etc. , etc. Here's a picture, she was one hot looking woman."

Parker looked at the picture and gave a low whistle, "Man, you aren't kidding. She was a knockout. So then what happened?"

"Then while out on their yacht, the husband ends up in the water and drowns. Mind you, this guy was on the swim team at college, even tried out for the Olympics, and an expert with boats. So how does he end up going overboard and drowning? There are all sorts of rumors that she killed him in a jealous rage since it turns out he was also quite the playboy. Charlotte gets worried about being charged with murder and hightails it back to the states. I bet daddy also bought off whoever he needed to save his little girl. Oh, and if that isn't enough, guess who's shoulder she cries on during this tragedy- none other than her dead hubby's best friend and schoolmate, Victor Pierce."

"Are you kidding me?" Parker was stunned. "This case keeps getting weirder by the minute."

"Yep, Miss Charlotte returns to the states, Victor is now in love with the poor dear and follows her. They get married after her father tries to warn him away. They have four kids, a nice but not glamorous life. Seems daddy also cut off the cash supply to try to get her to straighten out. From all appearances, Victor was a good husband. He worked hard to try to keep her happy, but without the money she was accustomed to having at her disposal she eventually gets bored and starts having affairs and files for divorce. The rest I believe you already know. Oh, except that she was also a suspect in her father's death. Officially he had a heart attack, but those that knew Charlotte said they had a huge argument and then he keeled over. People blamed her for the heart attack; God knows if she was my daughter I'd have one, too."

"Seriously? She really was a piece of work, people end up dead everywhere she goes, I'm surprised her kids are still alive. It's almost karma that she ends up with her head bashed in. All that money and it still isn't enough. I guess I'm lucky I'm just a poor detective. "

"I don't know I'd still take the money," laughed Kenny. "Give me a chance with yachts and beautiful women looking for a good time."

"In your dreams," Parker responded. "Good job on that information. Now if we can just get a break on this case. I think this one will haunt me for quite a while."

"Speaking of haunting, how's your buddy Squirrel these days?" Kenny inquired.

"Doing good, hopefully once this case is solved Kate and I will get together with him and Sarah."

Kenny glanced at Parker, "Sounds like things are getting more serious with you and the lovely ME. How's Karen taking it?"

"Karen is not happy, she called the other day. I reminded her we are through and she needs to live her own life. I just wish she'd find someone else and move on. It's too stressful dealing with her, and I have enough stress with this case."

"Good luck with that," Kenny said, "I've got to head out and see what else I can uncover. Maybe we'll get that lucky break. Catch you later."

"Ok, bye." Parker sat down at his desk and stared at the wall. Sighing, he opened his notes and started going over them again, looking for any clues he may have overlooked.

Several hours later, Parker looked up as someone called his name and saw Stella standing in the doorway. "I have Charles's number and address for you. I was coming into town and figured I'd drop it off."

Parker stood as Stella entered the room, "Thank you, why don't you have a seat? I was just going over some background history and maybe you can help fill me in."

Stella looked dubiously at Parker, "Well, I don't know how much help I can be." Parker waived her in and held out a seat.

"Please, this shouldn't take long." Still hesitant, Stella finally came forward and sat in the chair Parker held for her.

"Ok, what would you like to know?" she asked.

"Let's start with Charlotte's family if you can, what was her relationship like with her father and half- brother?" Parker looked expectantly at Stella, who took a deep breath before answering.

"Oh boy. Let's see. Like I said, this isn't my family history so I may not know enough to help you. Charlotte's father, Thomas, was married for a short time to his first wife. I don't know her name, but she died giving birth to Charles. Thomas remarried quickly, I guess to give Charles a mother, and a few years later Charlotte was born. From what I gather, Thomas was old school. He doted on his son, and pretty much ignored his daughter. Charles, being the son, was raised to take over the family business and carry on the legacy. Charlotte, being the daughter, was to be spoiled and married off to a nice, wealthy family. I don't know too much about Charles. I don't remember hearing much about him, I have never met him. I don't know if they got along or not. I'm guessing not or maybe we'd have heard more about him. I think Charlotte was in Europe, going to school, when her mom passed away. She flew back but got home too late. I think she felt guilt over not getting home in time, but Graham might know more about that. He is more of the family historian. "

"So what happened after her mother died? She returned to Europe and married, didn't she?" Parker asked.

"Yes, she went back to Europe and married Phillipe. I want to say they were only married about a year when he drowned, but I don't really know. No one knows what happened that night. The rumor is she killed him, but for some reason I just don't feel that she did. I don't know why, but I just don't see her doing that. I mean, why? Even if he was a playboy, she wasn't exactly the monogamous type herself, so I don't know what to think. I know there was an investigation of some sort, but her father was so rich I am sure things got resolved pretty quick and she was shipped back to the states."

"What about her second husband? And can I get you anything to drink; soda, water?"

"Water would be great, thanks," Stella responded. "Victor was Phillipe's best friend. I think he was in love with Charlotte from the first time he met her. How could he not be, she was so beautiful and vivacious. Still, he was the best man at her wedding, and after the accident, he followed Charlotte back here and ended up marrying her. I don't remember how long they were married, but I know her father was opposed to the marriage.

I don't know if it was because Victor wasn't from a wealthy family or what, but Thomas didn't want them getting married. Victor became a very successful businessman. He worked his way up from the bottom to the top of the company. Thomas cut Charlotte off financially when she married Victor. But after Victor started moving up at his company they did quite well, not like her father's money, but they weren't hurting. They had the kids and things were ok, but I guess Charlotte got bored being a housewife and mother. She was used to traveling to all sorts of exotic places and having all these adventures. I don't know for sure since I never asked her, but I'm sure part of it was after having all these men chasing her, being married and a mother just wasn't doing it for her anymore. I think she missed and craved the attention.

Anyway, she ended up leaving Victor. From what I'm told, she picked up her love life where she left off before she got married, eventually having Jonathan. She kept the pregnancy secret. Back in those days it wasn't socially acceptable to have a child out of wedlock. Her father never accepted the kid and I think that caused a lot of strife between them. It seems as though her mental state started really spiraling out of control after Jonathan was born. I know Victor tried his damnedest to get custody of the kids. Thomas even hired a private detective to try and find something to help get custody. The weird thing is, Victor was pretty powerful in his own right, and Thomas had plenty of money and power, and yet Charlotte retained custody. Go figure. I don't know if Victor just gave up after he remarried and Thomas died, no one has said what happened."

"Thomas died of a heart attack, is that correct?" Parker got up to replenish Stella's water, then sat down again.

"Yes, that is what I heard. Supposedly he and Charlotte got into a very heated argument and he died. People blame her of course. But once again, she is the only one who really knows what happened that night, and now she's gone, too."

"Tell me about the children, what happened with them?"

"Funny hearing you call them children," Stella smiled, "Let's see, after the divorce all the kids were sent to boarding schools. I think they were pretty upset about it at the time. They were still dealing with the upheaval of the divorce. But I think in the long run it was a good decision, as they all turned out to be well educated and successful. Charlotte took off for Europe for a bit while the kids were away, but after she came back and had Jonathan I think she stayed home."

"You said they all turned out to be successful, what do they do?" Parker inquired.

"Jake followed a similar career path as Victor. He became CEO, though of a different company. He was doing quite well, but I think he recently ran into some trouble at work and may actually be out of a job. I think the board of directors decided he wasn't doing what he should be doing as well as they would like, and are trying to get him fired. I don't know all the details. You'd have to ask Jake or Gina. Jake is extremely smart, so I don't think he'll be down for long. Whatever is going on may blow over, too. Graham is a partner in an investment house. We also have the horse business. I train, show horses, and teach riding. "

"And the girls?"

"Ellen works for a charity. Her first husband was a lawyer, and she made out quite well when they got divorced. Her current husband, Daniel, is more of a dreamer. I don't even know what his job is supposed to be. From what we can tell, all he does is drink and gamble. We were surprised this marriage has lasted. They were separated for a while, but they reconciled. Emily and her roommate Gail own a bar-restaurant that is doing quite well. They work a lot of hours, but it seems to be paying off, and that is not an easy business to own. But both of them are so outgoing and have such big, fun personalities which make the place a fun place to hang out. Plus the food is very good."

"This has been very helpful. What do you know about Jonathan and his wife?"

"Ah yes, Jonathan and Kelly, the golden couple. Both are extremely good looking, which of course they know. They are also manipulative, greedy, lying, assholes."

Parker smiled, "I can tell you aren't exactly fans of theirs."

"Not even close. I saw the way they treated Charlotte. They were so obviously in it for the money, and yet she repeatedly would buy their bullshit and think they loved her. They didn't care about her at all. Charlotte and I had our differences. But even as difficult as she could be, she didn't deserve to be treated like that. Some of the others will probably disagree because she raised Jonathan to be like that, but still, it isn't right. They are nothing but phonies and I don't trust a word they say. I don't know what he does for a living, I think he just mooches off of Charlotte. She funded a number of businesses over the years that he would start, and then give up on. He always had an excuse why they didn't work out, but the truth is he was just lazy. It got to the point where I doubt he ever even started any real business. I think he just fed her lines so she would continue to send him money. I can't believe she didn't see it. And there have been times I think she did it because she was afraid of him. He might seem smooth and debonair, but he has a mean streak a mile wide."

"Let me ask you this, do you think either one killed her?" Parker watched closely for Stella's reaction.

"I honestly don't know. I wouldn't put it past either one. But I guess as much as I don't trust them, I hate to believe they would kill her. She was his mom for crying out loud. How can a child kill their parent? I know it happens all the time, but still."

Parker thought a moment, then asked, "What about the others? Jake is known for his temper and is having money issues. Ellen and her husband also have issues. What is your feeling there?"

"Like I said, this is their mom. Even though the woman could drive you up a wall and make you tear your hair out, I don't see it. I guess if they were desperate enough. I know there have been plenty of times they have all asked her for money to bail them out of whatever financial mess they got into to, and sometimes she would turn them down to try to make a point of being more responsible. Which is sort of amusing when you consider she has been able to live her life the way she wanted without ever having to worry about money. It was handed to her. She never worked a day in her life. Her kids might be financially irresponsible, but at least they all work. The only one who never asked or received anything from her is Graham. He refused to give her the satisfaction. He is good with money, so he's never asked for a dime. This way she couldn't own him like she owned the others. Actually, I think if any of her four original kids were going to kill her, they would have done it years ago, and not because of the money, but her actions in dealing with them."

"Did you kill Charlotte?"

"No. That's not to say we got along, we didn't, though she could be nice, and even generous on occasion. My way of dealing with her was to avoid her as much as possible. Graham had to deal with her more because he is her son, and lived so close. But it did get to where he had to think of her as someone else, not his mother, or the pain of how she treated him was too difficult."

"What about boyfriends? Was she dating anyone?"

"Well, like Graham said, not that we were aware. She had several here over the years that I've known, but in the past couple of years, I don't remember any. At least not that she's mentioned. As you probably noticed, she was pretty secretive with her life so it's possible she was seeing someone, and just didn't tell us. I hope that helps with the investigation, but I really need to get going." Stella stood and prepared to leave.

"This has been a help, thank you for stopping by. If you think of anything else, please call me and let me know." Parker escorted Stella to the door, where she stopped and turned to face him.

"I know you have to look at those closest to the victim first, but I really think you need to think outsiders, too. Yes, there are several, if not most family members with a reason to want her dead, but I don't know. I can't help but feel the answer is elsewhere, unless Jonathan and Kelly decided not to wait any longer to get the money."

"What do you mean?"

"She left everything to Jonathan. I think it's like fifteen million. No one but Graham knew about that. He was afraid to tell the others because he knew they'd go ballistic. Jake of course is already contesting it, so it will be messy for quite some time, I'm sure."

"But, at the time she was murdered, only Graham knew, the others still thought they were getting the money, is that correct?"

"Yes, I suppose so. But remember, the assumption was the estate was going to be divided equally, among the five children, plus I'm sure she left a bunch to a variety of charities and that kind of thing. The amount would have been maybe three million apiece. I know, that is still not exactly chump change but remember Detective, these folks were all getting money from her on a regular basis. And over the years they stood to gain significantly more if she was alive. I still don't see them doing it, and I'm sure they have solid alibis. The only one that I wouldn't be surprised to find out is a murderer, is Jonathan. He knew about the will and as far as I'm concerned, he had fifteen million reasons to kill her." Stella and Parker looked at each other for a few moments before Stella turned and walked out the door.

Parker thought about what Stella had told him. It was true, the alibis were checking out, though some were only verified by a spouse, so that could change. He also agreed for the most part that except for Jonathan or Kelly, the children didn't feel right. Still, he wasn't quite ready to cross anyone off the list just yet. He remembered something a seasoned detective told him about solving homicides. "When you are in a field of ponies, don't look for the unicorn," Parker said out loud. Well, he was definitely in a field of ponies. It was time to start looking a bit deeper at Jonathan and Kelly.

Stella stopped her bike and contemplated the turn. It was a tight, downhill left-hand switchback, with roots running across the middle. She had previously been able to ride it, but lately the roots had become more pronounced and after nearly crashing once, she was now wary of trying it. While she pondered the best way to do it, she heard another rider approaching. She moved her bike off to the side to allow the other rider to pass, but he stopped when he reached her. Stella recognized Kenny Mann and said hi.

"You're Detective Mann, right?"

"Yes," Kenny answered. "The best way to do that is like a circumcision."

Stella was a bit startled. "Excuse me?"

"The turn, take it wide and cut off the tip. Here, watch." Kenny rode his bike around the turn and stopped. "Try it. Take it wide to the right, head towards the rock and roll on by."

Stella was dubious, but gave it a try, knees shaking as she started the turn.

"Remember to look in the direction you want to go," Kenny called out.

Stella rolled around the turn, heart pounding, but made it cleanly. Stopping next to Kenny she breathed a sigh of relief and smiled.

"That helped, thanks."

"No problem. Where is your husband, is he riding, too?" Kenny asked.

Taking a sip of water, Stella responded, "He's here, way up ahead somewhere. He likes going faster than I do, and has more talent so this stuff doesn't bother him. I've had too many horse related injuries so I'm always leery of getting hurt. Plus, he doesn't exactly have any patience for teaching me stuff. It's like husbands teaching wives to drive."

Kenny smiled and said, "I don't mind teaching. I like to encourage people to get out and ride. Anytime you need help, just give me a call and I'll be glad to come ride with you. Your husband, of course. I don't want him to get the wrong idea."

"Well, it would depend on his mood at any rate, which lately hasn't been so wonderful." Stella looked off at the trees for a moment before looking back at Kenny. "I am trying to deal with it, and remember that his mother was murdered, and the killer is still out there, but he's not making it easy. It's like one minute he's upbeat and normal, then I say something and he turns into Cujo. I feel like I'm constantly walking on eggshells around him."

Kenny looked at Stella, "I'm sorry to hear that, though it's not unusual in these situations. Is there anything I can do to help?"

"Find the killer," she replied. "And thanks again for the help. I may take you up on that offer," she said as she started pedaling again, heading down the trail.

Kenny watched her go, and then decided to turn around and take a different trail. He didn't want to bump into her again just yet, especially not if her husband was in a foul mood. *I can't wait for this case to be over,* he thought as he rode.

14 CHAPTER FOURTEEN

"Momma?" Charlotte softly entered the room where her mother laid in the bed, thin and pale, eyes closed and breathing raggedly. "Momma? I'm here, can you hear me? Momma? Please wake up, please don't die." Tears streamed down Charlotte's face as she held her mother's limp hand in hers. "Please momma, open your eyes. Momma, I'm so sorry for everything, I tried to be a good girl, I really did. I promise I'll try harder, just please wake up." Sobbing, Charlotte leaned over and hugged her mother one last time, as her mother's ragged breathing eventually stopped, and she lay still.

The next few days were a blur of visitors and funeral arrangements. Charlotte felt as though her entire world had died with her mother. The one person she felt closest to, who stood by her no matter what and sheltered her from her father. Charlotte was not particularly close to her older brother, he was too much like her father, always proper and concerned about appearances. She longed to get back to Paris, where she had been staying when she received word of her mother's illness and hurried home.

Charlotte was sitting in the drawing room of her parent's estate house when Thomas entered.

"How long are you staying?" he asked.

"Just until the funeral, then I'll be returning to Paris," Charlotte replied.

"Don't you think you should move back here?"

"Why? So you can parade me around like the good little daughter you care so much about? Stop pretending you love me, dad. I know your only concern is how people see us. If you only knew half of what goes on in Europe."

"Enough! It so happens I do love you, despite how it may seem to you. You better watch yourself young lady, how do you suppose you can afford to live in Europe? I should cut your funds off and make you come home. Maybe then you'd appreciate what I've done for you instead of behaving like a spoiled brat. Do you have any idea the pain you have caused us? Do you? Do you know how many nights your mother cried herself to sleep because you didn't write her, or come see her? Now you show up, when it's too late!" Thomas glared at his daughter, then turned and stormed towards the door.

"Go ahead! Cut off the money, I don't care!" Charlotte yelled at her father. *"Phillipe and I are getting married soon anyway and I won't need your money!"*

Thomas stopped and slowly turned to face his daughter. Staring daggers at her he responded *"Are you pregnant?"*

Charlotte gasped, and then glared back defiantly, *"Of course not, how dare you suggest that! It so happens that Phillipe and I are in love. That is the reason why we are getting married. "*

Thomas looked coolly at Charlotte, *"Your mother would have loved to plan a wedding for you. It's too bad you didn't tell her this before she died. I will have it all arranged."*

"No, it's already been taken care of. We are getting married as soon as I return to Paris. There is no need for you to get involved. "

"You are my only daughter, and I will not let you elope. You will be married here, and then you may return to Paris and do what you want. Until that time, you will do as I say. There will be no more discussion. Good night Charlotte." With that Thomas turned and walked out of the room, leaving Charlotte staring silently after him, tears running down her face.

"Oh mamma, why did you have to leave me? I'm sorry mamma, I'm so sorry," Charlotte sobbed as she sank into a chair.

15 CHAPTER FIFTEEN

Jonathan hung up the phone and stared out the window. Detective Williams was becoming a pain in the ass. How many times does he have to tell him where he was and what he was doing around the time of his mother's murder already? The guy just won't let up. It was beginning to make him nervous. What if he keeps digging? No telling what he will discover, and there is plenty that should probably be left alone. Jonathan thought about the recent troubles in his marriage. He and Kelly had separated, with Kelly going to live in Florida, working for a guy that made porn movies. Of course he told everyone she was modeling, but somehow his brothers and sisters discovered what the truth was. There were some ugly times when they realized his and Kelly's young daughter was living in the guy's house with Kelly. An anonymous tip had led them to something written online and the details were not pretty. After social services got wind of the situation, and began investigating how their daughter was being raised, Kelly fled Florida and came back to Jonathan, begging forgiveness. It took a lot of counseling, but so far things were ok. It wasn't like Jonathan was a saint, either. He kept hidden the child he had after a fling with another woman while Kelly was away.

Even Kelly didn't know about the kid. *Lord help me if she ever finds out,* he thought. I guess it's a good thing mom is dead; she would have had a fit if she knew any of this, though she wasn't exactly little miss prim and proper herself. Look at all the skeletons in her closet. Hell, look at him, one of the biggest of them all.

Daniel opened another beer and walked into the living room where Ellen sat staring out the window.

"So how was the funeral?" he asked.

"Everyone wanted to know where you were. I wish you had been there with me, I could have used the support." Ellen turned to face her husband.

Daniel took another sip of his beer. Tall, thin with thinning blond hair falling to his shoulders and plain features on a long face, no one would describe him as handsome. "I'm sure no one really cared whether or not I was there. It's no secret I'm not exactly welcome in your family, especially where your mother was concerned. "

"You still should have been there out of respect for me and my mother." Ellen countered.

"What? And be a hypocrite? Everyone knew your mother and I couldn't stand each other. I seriously doubt she would want me at her funeral pretending I was sad she's gone. That woman was hateful. I'm sorry she was your mother, but that's the way it goes."

"You are such a prick. You could at least show some concern for me and my loss!" Ellen screamed at her husband.

"Of course I feel sorry for you, I know she was your mother, but give me a break already!" Daniel chugged his beer and stormed back to the kitchen to open another one. "At least now you can get your inheritance and we can get out of all this debt."

"The reason we are in debt is because of you and your bad ideas, gambling and drinking! Maybe if you didn't drink so much you could finish the jobs you start and we might get paid! Besides, we aren't getting any inheritance, mom left everything to Jonathan."

Daniel stopped in his tracks as he was coming back in the living room. "What did you say? What do you mean she left everything to Jonathan? You're her daughter who she always said she loved so much, she had to leave you something!" Daniel stared at Ellen.

"Well, guess what, if you were hanging around waiting on a nice, big payoff when she died, you are out of luck. Now take your beer and get out of my face. I don't want to look at you anymore. Everyone told me you were just hanging with me for the money. I can't believe I used to defend you. Now get out of here and let me mourn my mother by myself." Daniel walked over to Ellen and tried to put his arms around her.

"Aw come on honey, you know I love you. You're just saying that because you're upset, you don't really mean it. Why don't you take a nice, hot bath and go lie down. You've had a rough day, I know. I'll fix something for you to eat and we can talk in the morning." With that, Daniel gently pulled Ellen off the couch and led her upstairs.

"MOM!" Emily screamed as she jumped out of the bed. Her

heart pounding, blood running like ice through her veins, eyes wide, Emily stared in the darkness at the figure standing in front of her, before it suddenly vanished.

"What is it?" Gail asked. "Emily, what's wrong?" Gail sat up in the bed and turned on the light. "Emily, talk to me!"

Emily turned her ashen face to her lover, shaking like a leaf in the wind. "I just saw my mom." She said her voice unsteady. "She was right here, in this room. I could see her. She was trying to tell me something, but I couldn't hear what she was saying."

Gail stared at Emily, "Are you saying you saw a ghost? Are you sure it wasn't just a dream? With all the stress you've been under, it was probably just a nightmare."

Emily shook her head as she sat back on the bed. "This was no dream, believe me. I saw my mom. I'm so freaked out right now, I can't believe it. Why is she showing up? What is she trying to tell me?"

Gail brushed her long, auburn hair out of her face and sighed. "I'm sure it was just a nightmare Emily. Your mother isn't going to start haunting people. Come on back to bed and try to get some sleep, you need your rest."

Emily shook her head, "I know what I saw and I'm telling you Gail, it was no nightmare. She was standing right by the end of the bed, trying to say something. Then she just vanished. My heart is still racing just thinking about it, look, I still have goose bumps on my arms."

"Ok, then as long as we can't sleep, let's go downstairs and have a cup of tea, come on." Gail got out of bed and putting her arm around Emily's shoulders, led her down the stairs. Once they reached the kitchen, Gail set a pot of water on the stove to boil as Emily got out the cups, sugar and tea bags and set them on the table. Leaning against the counter, she ran a hand through her short, dark, hair, her fingers getting tangled in the curls. "Man, I wish I had your hair, I hate these curls. I've always wanted long, straight hair, instead of this mop on my head." Gail smiled and said, her voice soft, with an Australian accent, "I think your curls are marvelous. I've always wanted curly hair, I am never able to do much with mine, especially in the humidity, it just goes flat. Here, have your tea," she said pouring the boiling water in the cups. "Here's to your mum," Gail lifted her cup in a toast and took a sip. "I'm sorry I didn't get to know her better."

Emily sipped her tea and replied, "You know that wasn't possible, we couldn't take a chance on her knowing about us. I wanted her to like you, and as long as you were just a roommate, she did. There is no telling what she would have done if she found out we are lovers. I just couldn't risk it."

"I know, but I hate living a lie like that. Now that she's gone, why can't we be out in the open? Who cares what anyone thinks? I love you and want to let the world know."

"I know, it's just that my family is complicated, to say the least. I love you, too. Just give me a little time, ok?" Emily leaned over and took Gail's hands in hers. "It will all work out, I promise." Gail looked at Emily and smiled.

"Ok. Now let's go back to bed, it's late and I have to work tomorrow. No more visits from your mum, either. That was enough excitement for one night," she said her hand tousling Emily's curls as they headed back to the bedroom.

Graham slid his weight back a bit on the bike seat. Racing down the windy singletrack, the 29 inch wheels on his mountain bike soaking up the bumps as he flew over the rocks, Graham relished the feeling of being on the edge. Just a slight misjudgment on the trail would send him crashing to the ground. Graham loved the adrenaline rush he got from riding the bike. The faster he could go along, sweeping through the turns, grinding it up the hills, bombing down the descents, wind whistling past his ears, it was an amazing feeling. The thrill of being able to negotiate the roots, rocks and log overs was a total rush. All too soon he came to the bottom of the descent and stopped to wait on Stella, who was far more cautious. The idea of going that fast and risk breaking another bone wasn't so appealing. Stella enjoyed a slightly slower pace, at least through the loose, rocky sections of the trails. Catching up to Graham, Stella stopped and looked at him. "Do you have a death wish or something? You are insane to go that fast on that trail. One of these days you are going to crash and kill yourself." Graham just smiled.

"Nah, it's just such a rush, and it lets me forget everything else since I have to concentrate so much on not crashing."

"You are nuts." Stella replied. "But I'll admit that was fun. Now, let's see who can keep up," she said as she took off pedaling madly ahead of Graham. Graham laughed and followed, eventually catching and passing Stella to lead the way. They rode for another hour before coming out onto a different trail.

"Wait a minute, isn't this the spot where your mom was killed?" Stella slowed and came to a stop, looking at Graham with a puzzled expression. "Why do you want to ride here?"

"I need to see where it happened," Graham replied. "I don't know why, I can't explain it, but I just feel I need to be here. Who knows, maybe we'll find something that will help with the investigation."

Stella shook her head. "I think it's creepy. But if you want to do this, ok." Getting got off the bikes, they walked around a bit until they found a spot that was still showing signs of where the ground had been trampled around the crime scene. Neither spoke as they stood staring at the ground. Suddenly they both jumped as a voice behind them said "Hello". Both turned to see Parker Williams standing behind them, leaning on his mountain bike.

"I'm surprised to see you two here," he said. "I wouldn't think you'd want to ride here."

Graham looked at Parker and replied, "I had to see where it happened. I'm not even sure why. I guess just to get some sort of closure. Have you gotten anywhere with the investigation yet? Do you have any credible suspects?"

"We're still following up leads and doing our investigation. Can you think of anything else that you might have forgotten that could help us?"

"Nothing comes to mind," said Graham. Stella shook her head.

"Tell me about your mother. You said she wasn't she always crazy?"

Graham thought a moment before responding. "No, from what I heard from relatives, and when we were very young, she was beautiful, vivacious, fun, and outgoing. She lived and went to school abroad. Her father always felt the schools in Europe were far superior to even the best schools here. Mom apparently had a ton of friends. Men were always chasing after her, and she was the belle of the ball as they say. I think it all started after her first husband's death. They were only married a short time. I think it was only about a year or so. I'm not sure since she never talked about it. I don't know what happened, but there was talk she killed him. All I know is from what I heard. She wasn't the same when she came home. It wasn't long before she married my dad, had us, got bored and got divorced. Dad used to say he felt something wasn't right, like she never got over the stigma of Phillipe's death. Who knows, maybe she did kill him and the guilt got her. More likely it was the loss of the lifestyle she had always known .You get labeled a killer and your "friends" drop you. I don't think her ego could handle it. It was like she needed people to like her to justify her existence."

Graham stared off at the trees and continued.

"There are also those that think it started with her mother's death, and that may be, too. I think her mother kept her in check, and made her feel loved. Her father was not one to demonstrate any affection, he was pretty cold. I think losing her mother got her started on the free love lifestyle she fell into. Then of course things really started going downhill when she got pregnant with Jonathan. Trying to hide that from everyone I think is what really started her slide into mental illness. You just can't live that big a lie and not have repercussions."

"Thanks Graham, that is helpful. I know this hasn't been easy on you and we will do our best to find who did this and bring them to justice. If you think of anything at all, no matter how trivial, call me. You never know what might turn out to be important." With that Parker got on his bike and headed back towards the trail head. Graham and Stella watched as he rode away.

"Well, that was creepy." Stella said.

"Sure was. Let's go back to the truck. I've had enough for one day." Graham replied as he got on his bike and headed back the way they came.

16 CHAPTER SIXTEEN

Charlotte stood at the side of the field watching the men on their horses as they chased the ball across the field. She never really understood polo. In fact she didn't even like the game, but there was a certain power and sexiness about it that drew her in. It didn't take her long to pick out Miguel, he had arrogance in his riding that stood out among the other riders. The effortless way he rode, making it seem as though he and his horse were one. "That is why he is one of the best players in the world," she mused. Charlotte looked down at the small boy standing quietly beside her. He was intently watching the game, dark eyes lighting up as the horses galloped across the field.

Charlotte smiled at her son, "It's exciting, isn't it?"

Jonathan looked up at his mother, smiling wide, his face glowing. "Can I do that someday?"

"You can do whatever you like honey," Charlotte smiled back.

On the field, the game over, the men rode back to the side of the field where the grooms waited to take the horses. Miguel gracefully dismounted and with an easy gait, walked towards the cars. Suddenly he stopped as he spotted Charlotte standing nearby.

"Well, Charlotte, long time no see. What are you doing here?" he asked as he slowly approached.

"I wanted you to meet your son," Charlotte replied. "Jonathan, say hello to your father."

"Hello sir," Jonathan dutifully replied.

"My son? I thought you were taking care of that situation!" Miguel hissed at Charlotte. "What do you want from me?"

"As you can see, the "situation" as you call it, is very much alive. I don't need or want anything from you other than to recognize your own flesh and blood. A child needs to know who his father is. Look, can't we talk someplace else?"

Miguel gave a short, harsh laugh, "The last time we talked someplace else, you told me you were pregnant and almost ran me over. What other surprises have you in store for me?"

"Well, I can assure you I am not pregnant this time," Charlotte replied haughtily.

Miguel snorted and stared down at Jonathan. "I suppose he does resemble me."

"Are you implying you think it's someone else's child?" Charlotte glared. "How dare you!"

"Well, it's not like I was your only lover. As I recall, you were quite popular," Miguel gave a short laugh.

"That doesn't mean I was sleeping with any of them! That was just a hateful thing to say, but what else I can expect from you."

Just then a beautiful, sharply dressed woman approached. "Miguel *darling, are you ready?"*

"Yes, my love. I was just talking to an old friend. Charlotte, this is my wife, Melanie. Melanie, this is Charlotte. I used to play for her father years ago. Now Charlotte, it was nice to see you again, but we really must be going. Come along dear." Miguel took Melanie's arm as they walked past Charlotte and headed to their car.

Jonathan looked up at his mother, "Mommy, doesn't Daddy like me? Why didn't he talk to us? Is he mad at me?"

"No honey," she said as she bent down to give him a hug. "He's just an asshole. Come on, I guess we may as well go see your grandfather, he's waiting."

Charlotte pulled into the drive of her father's beach house and parked the car. She sat for a moment before taking a deep breath and got out of the car. Picking up Jonathan, she walked up the sidewalk and into the house.

"Father, I'm here," She called out as she walked towards the library.

"Well, what do we have here?" Thomas rose from behind his desk, walking over to give Charlotte a quick embrace before standing back and looking at Jonathan.

"This is Jonathan," she responded. "Jonathan, this is your grandfather. Jonathan is the one I adopted. I thought it about time you met."

"Yes, I remember. Adopted." Thomas stared at his daughter, and then motioned her to the couch. "Have a seat and we can discuss this. Jonathan, go with Lucy while I talk to your mother. Lucy, come take Jonathan and make him some lunch."

Lucy, one of the staff in the house, came and took Jonathan by the hand, leading him off to the kitchen.

"Now, about this adoption of yours. I have my own suspicions. You might as well tell me the truth. I had a private detective following you after your divorce, if you recall. He had some interesting things to report. You are an irresponsible, divorced woman with four kids you can't afford without my help. There is no way in hell anyone will let you adopt a child. Therefore, who is this child, and who is the father?"

"I already told you, he's adopted! Are you implying I had a child out of wedlock? Who do you think I am?"

"Charlotte! Cut the crap, I know your reputation and I've seen for myself how you conduct yourself with men. I just thank God your mother didn't live to see this, she would be so ashamed!"

"Stop it! Don't you bring mother into this!" Charlotte was on her feet screaming at her father.

"Why couldn't you be more like your brother, he's never given me an ounce of trouble. You, on the other hand, are nothing but trouble. I send you to the finest schools in Europe, and what happens? You marry some playboy and then push him off the yacht. Then you marry Victor, who treats you like gold, but that isn't enough for you and you leave. Now you show up with some brat you claim you adopted when we all know it's bullshit. How did you manage to hide it? That's what I want to know, that and who the father is. It's that polo player, isn't it? The detective followed you and I have pictures of you two together. Does he want money to keep it quiet?" Thomas was standing in front of his daughter, yelling, his face red with rage.

Charlotte broke down in tears, screaming back at her father. "He's not a brat! Fine, he's my child, ok? Are you happy now?! You want the truth? I'll give you the truth! You're right, I was screwing Miguel, and he's the father! I also screwed my way all over Europe, and do you know why? I was looking for a man that would love me, for who I am, one that would hold me, and care for me and tell me he loved me. Not like my father, who only cares about appearances, and that his little angelic daughter behave like the proper lady and keep her knees closed and marry some stuffed shirt with a mistress on the side so that he doesn't look bad. You don't give a crap about me, you never have! You only care that I don't suck it up and pretend to be the obedient little child you want like my brother!"

"I gave you EVERYTHING you ungrateful little brat! How dare you say I don't love you! You have broken my heart time and time again behaving like the self-centered, spoiled brat you are! Your problem is your mother let you get away with everything; she was too soft on you. At least she raised Charles correctly. He's turned out to be someone I can be proud of."

"Here we go again with your precious Charles. Well Daddy dearest, let me tell you something else about my wonderful, perfect brother. That wonderful son you brag so much about? He raped me when I was twelve! That whole summer was hell, and where were you to protect me, huh? Where? He got me drunk and then he raped me, and you did NOTHING to protect me! Why do you think I agreed to go to Europe, it was to get away from him! And not only that, Charles was the one who pushed Phillipe off the yacht, not me! He was insanely jealous that I got married and he couldn't screw me anymore! That's right; your precious, perfect son from your precious, perfect wife, is a child molester and a killer!" Charlotte screamed, tears streaming down her face.

"LIAR! You would stoop that low to accuse your brother of that, you mean little bitch!" Thomas' face was purple as he screamed back at

Charlotte.

"It's true, and he's not my brother, he's my half-brother! Go ahead, ask him, ask him what's it's like to screw your sister, ask him about watching me get dressed and sneaking into my room! I should report him to the authorities and have him arrested, and then what would all your friends think!"

Thomas slapped Charlotte across the face with such force it knocked her to the floor.

"Get out! Get out and don't ever come back! And take your bastard child with you! I am taking you out of my will, you are no longer my daughter! You are a lying whore and I will not have anything to do with you any longer!" Thomas exploded with rage at his daughter.

Sobbing, Charlotte slowly got off the floor, "All I ever wanted was for you to love me, was that asking so much? WAS IT? All you ever cared about was Charles! I hate you, I hate you, I hate you! I hope you die!" she screamed as she ran out of the library, slamming the door behind her. Thomas stared after her for a moment, and then suddenly buckled to his knees as the pain in his chest hit him like a ton of bricks. "Charlotte, help!" he gasped as the pain increased and he sank to the floor. "Help," he softly moaned before his heart finally gave out, and stopped beating.

17 CHAPTER SEVENTEEN

"Did I tell you I saw Mom's ghost the other night? She was standing at the foot of my bed, scared the living crap out of me. I swear she was trying to tell me something, but I just don't know what it was," Emily was helping Ellen making dinner at Ellen's house.

"Are you sure it wasn't a dream?" Ellen looked over at her sister.

"It was no dream, it was real all right. I've been waiting to see if she returns. What if she is trying to tell me who the killer is? Maybe we should do a séance or something."

Ellen stopped chopping the apples she was adding to the salad. "Are you nuts? There is no way we are doing that!"

"But what if that is the only way we find out who killed her? Don't you want to know?"

"Know what?" Daniel asked as he walked in the room.

"Emily thinks she saw Mom's ghost and that Mom is trying

to tell her who murdered her. She wants to do a séance."

Daniel paled a bit and looked at the two women. "That's not a good idea at all. Besides, the police are handling it. That detective keeps asking all sorts of questions, he will probably figure it out."

Ellen looked quizzically at her husband, "What do you mean he keeps asking questions? Do you mean he keeps interviewing you? Why? Do you know something you aren't telling us?"

"Yeah, Daniel, you didn't kill her, did you?" laughed Emily.

"What? No, of course not, it's just that he says he's still investigating and has things to follow up on. You mean he hasn't been asking you guys the same things?"

"Well, he has talked to us a few times, so maybe that's all it is. I just wish he'd solve it, I mean, what if it was one of us, or someone we know? It creeps me out to think we could be talking to that person every day and not know they killed our mother," Emily shivered. "I tell you one thing, if she shows up again; I'm going to ask her who did it."

"I can just see you in court now, telling the judge you heard it from your dead mother," laughed Ellen. "And come on, do you really think one of us would do it?"

"Well, I'd be willing to bet every one of us has thought of it, or at least thought about her being dead. Look at what she has done to us. I know my blood pressure goes up when she gets on one of her rants."

Daniel grabbed another beer from the refrigerator and leaned against the counter. "I don't think you should joke about things like that. The last thing I need is your mother showing up and haunting me. She was difficult enough to deal with when she was alive."

"Oh come on Daniel, lighten up. We're just trying to throw a little levity into the situation. God knows, she could pluck your last nerve, but she was still our mother and we loved her." Ellen finished with the salad, setting it on the table. "Now everyone sit down and enjoy lunch. Emily, don't forget to get something to drink, Daniel and I already have ours."

Emily poured some water into a glass and sat down. "You know what else I've been wondering? Why wasn't Uncle Charles at the funeral? Has anyone even heard from him?"

"He and Mom were estranged, remember? They haven't seen each other in years. I don't remember why, if she even told us the reason."

"I know, but still, this is his only sister, you would think he'd at least call or something, unless of course, no one told him. Do you think we should contact him and let him know?" Emily asked.

"Half-sister. You know, I have no idea if he was told or not. Maybe Graham knows. I was so upset at the time, and with Uncle Charles not being in the picture much, I never even thought about him. "

"Maybe I'll ask Graham about it tomorrow, maybe he has an address or phone number for Charles, as well." The three of them continued eating their lunch, the conversation ebbing and flowing as they ate.

18 CHAPTER EIGHTEEN

Kate stared dubiously at the bike, then at Parker. "So you tell me I'm supposed to ride this thing in the woods? Where are the training wheels?"

"That is correct and there are none," Parker replied. "You said you rode a bike before. You know that saying, it's just like riding a bike. So, grab the handles, squeeze the brake levers to hold it steady, and hop on."

Kate grabbed the handles as she was told and carefully sat on the bike.

"Ok, I can do this," she muttered under her breath, "nice and easy."

"You do know at some point you will need to put both feet on the pedals, right?" Parker chuckled. "When you are ready, take a deep breath, and start pedaling. We'll just stay on the paved part for now, until you get more comfortable. Trust me, this will be fun."

"Sure it will, I've heard that before. Let's hope I don't have so much fun I end up in the emergency room."

"Don't worry, I will take good care of you, besides, I can't have some ER doctor with his hands on you."

Kate laughed and putting her feet on the pedals, started off down the paved path, a bit wobbly at first, before straightening out.

"Hey look, I'm doing it!" she laughed as she pedaled along. "You're right. It is just like riding..oops!" Kate almost ran off the path, but steered herself back on.

"Now do you remember what I told you about shifting? Try it out and make sure you shift smoothly. Don't push hard on the pedals at the same time, or you could end up with chain suck. Which believe me, you don't want. That's it, now practice shifting to a harder gear, and back down to an easier one as we go along. You want to be able to figure out where you feel comfortable. And if the pedaling starts getting too easy or too hard, shift up or down until it feels right. You kind of want to stay spinning at the same pace."

"You didn't tell me it would be this complicated, or that I would be this sore already, what's with this seat? How come I don't have one of those nice big, fat gel seats? This one is hard as a rock. My butt is killing me already!" Kate stopped the bike and stood up to stretch. "I don't know how you ride this thing like you do. I'm going to be so sore tomorrow, I probably won't be able to walk!"

"You'll get used to it, you just need to develop the muscles.

You'll see. After you get your own bike, you can get a different seat. But if you ride a lot, and you'll have to trust me on this, you'll want a seat like the one you are using today. Plus, if you wear bike shorts with the chamois, it helps. Why don't we ride up a bit further? There is a place we can stop and rest, and have the snacks I brought." Parker started pedaling again. "Oh, and quit whining!" he laughed.

Kate rolled her eyes, but got back on the bike and followed after Parker. About a mile down the path they came to an area where a few picnic tables were, overlooking the James River.

"This is such a pretty place," Kate said, as she got off and leaned the bike against the table. "We should do this more often."

Parker took the drinks and snacks they brought out of the backpack and set them on the table. "Yes, we should. Once you get the hang of riding, there are all sorts of cool places we can go. I have some favorite places, you will love them."

"Let's see if I can handle riding again before we get too crazy about this," Kate laughed as she opened her drink.

19 CHAPTER NINETEEN

Emily noticed the woman first. Standing at her mother's grave with her back to Emily, the stranger stood facing the headstone with her head bowed. She was average in height, slim, well dressed in jeans, a dark blouse, and cowboy boots. Her long grey hair, gathered in a ponytail, hung down her back. She turned and faced Emily, large, soft brown eyes in a friendly face. She bore a striking resemblance to the singer Melissa Etheridge, and could pass for a rock star herself. The woman smiled as Emily approached.

"You must be Emily," she said, her husky voice betrayed a bit of a foreign accent.

"I'm sorry, have we met?" Emily looked a bit confused.

"I'm Kiki Cassidy. I was a friend of your mother's," Kiki extended her hand to Emily.

"Kiki, of course! We've heard so much about you, I'm so glad to finally meet you!" Emily took her hand in both of hers. "I can't believe you're here. It's so weird that we're here at the same time."

"Maybe not," Kiki replied, "Let me ask you, were you planning on being here today?"

Emily looked puzzled, and then responded, "Actually no. I'm not even sure why I'm here today. I was going to come out later this week, but just had this strong feeling I should go visit Mom's grave. How did you know?"

Kiki looked straight into Emily's eyes and said, "She wanted you to come out here today. She has been visiting you, hasn't she?" Emily paled a bit and shook her head and stepped back.

"I don't know what you mean."

"I think you do, my dear. Your mother had abilities as it were. I know you've seen her, I can see it in your face. It's ok," she continued quickly as Emily looked ready to bolt, "I think we need to talk, there is a lot you need to hear about your mother. I haven't had lunch yet, is there somewhere we can go and have a bite to eat? You may even want a drink for this."

Emily was a bit stunned, her mind reeling, but finally replied, "Yes, I think a talk is in order. There is a nice, quiet place not too far from here, you can follow me."

Kiki smiled, "Please, lead the way."

The women were seated in the restaurant, having picked a booth away from other diners. After perusing the menu and placing their orders, Emily looked at Kiki.

"So."

Kiki smiled that warm, inviting smile, took a sip of her drink and placed it gently on the table. "So."

"Can you explain what you meant about my mother visiting me?" Emily wasn't quite sure what to make of Kiki, and was still a bit unnerved by their conversation at the cemetery.

"It's quite simple. Charlotte and I were very close, as you may know. There were many, many times when we knew what the other was thinking, without even saying it. Even though we didn't look at all alike, we were like twins in a lot of ways. Your mother and I still talked on a regular basis. We generally didn't let more than a couple of weeks go by without speaking. But, when we didn't speak, it was like we still knew what the other was doing, we were that close. Often I would call her and she would tell me she was just picking up the phone to call me. Or, the phone would ring and I'd know it was her, or I was just going to call her. Things like that would happen all the time.

Then one day, I was walking into my kitchen and I stopped. I stood there for several minutes, forgetting what it was I went in there for. This has never happened to me before. I had a very weird, bad feeling. I can't really even explain it. I felt such pain in my head and then dizzy, like I was going to pass out. My first thought was that maybe I was having a stroke, but then the feeling passed and there was just this emptiness I hadn't felt before. It was then I realized your mother was dead."

"Wait a minute, aren't you still living in England? How could you possibly know when she died?" Emily asked skeptically.

"Yes, I was in France at the time. Charlotte's and my

connection was so strong, it didn't have boundaries. You wanted to know how I knew she was visiting. Please let me explain."

"I'm sorry. It's just that this is freaking me out a bit, to say the least. Please continue."

"Once I realized she was gone, I sat down and just cried for hours. I didn't have anyone's contact information, so I couldn't call and speak to any of you. That night, after I went to bed, I woke up and saw Charlotte at the foot of my bed. I could tell she was trying to tell me something, but I couldn't tell what it was. She appeared several more times over the next week, though I still didn't know why. Remember, I had no idea what had happened to her, I only knew she had died. One morning after the last time she came to me, I got this overwhelming feeling I needed to be here. I booked a flight and came out. Once I was here, I found an article in the paper about the murder. I was then able to find where she was buried. I don't know why, but I knew one of her children would be here. And if they did show up, that meant she visited them, too, and made them come to her grave so we can meet."

Emily sat in stunned silence for a minute. "Holy crap. I can't believe this, wow. You are right, mom did show up. I couldn't tell what she wanted, either. It totally freaked me out, too. I told Ellen I was thinking of using the Ouija board or something to try to figure it out, but she talked me out of it," Emily took a long swallow on her drink.

"It's a good thing you listened, nothing good comes out of that board, that's a whole different bucket of worms. Your mother and I did that once, never again. But we'll save that story for another day." Kiki shook her head, then placed her hands on

Emily's hands, "Please promise me you won't do that, please."

"I won't, I promise. So if your assumption is correct, why do you think Mom wanted us to meet? And why me?" Emily sat her drink down, signaled to the waitress for another drink for herself, and one for Kiki.

Kiki thought for a moment before answering. "I probably knew your mother better than anyone. We met when she came to Europe to go to school. I don't know how much she told you and your siblings about those years, her childhood, or her first marriage, or anything that happened after the accident and her return to the States. I am sure you have questions and maybe I'm here to answer them. Maybe somewhere in here we can help discover why she was killed. Why did she show herself to you? I don't know, other than you may be the only one sensitive enough for her to get through. It's possible no one else could see her, so you're the lucky one."

"Mom, never talked much about her childhood, and she never talked about her first marriage. There are rumors she killed her first husband, but no one knows for sure. She did talk about you quite a bit. It sounded like you two had quite a blast over there, some of the stories she told were quite exciting."

Kiki laughed, "Yes, we did have quite a time. Did she ever tell you about the band we were in? She was something to see, she was so beautiful, and could she sing," Kiki sighed. "We would play various clubs all over the place. We caused quite a stir. We both had our hair really long, hers that very pretty blond, mine was dark brown. I played guitar and we both sang. We had such a great time. The guys in the band were great, and we even dated a couple of them. It was so exciting back then."

Emily was smiling, "She never told us about that. What happened to the band?"

Kiki's smile faded. "Charlotte's father didn't think the band lifestyle was appropriate. He told Charlotte he was going to cut her funds if she didn't quit the band and start living a more proper lifestyle. I know it's hard to imagine now, but back then it was unheard of for women to be in a band like ours. Rock and roll was just starting, and you didn't see women doing it. We were way ahead of our time. Thomas was furious. In his mind she was making a fool of herself and the family name, doing what she was doing. He was so stuck on appearances, but that was pretty typical of the super wealthy back then. Thomas had to be in control, and the only way he could do that was with his money. If he only tried using love instead, maybe things would have been different.

Charlotte was absolutely devastated. We both were, since the band wasn't as good without her. Your mother dreamed of making it as a singer. She loved being on the stage, loved the attention and the crowds loved her. She had a style that just captivated everyone. I really wish her father had understood how important it was to her, she seemed to change after that. I think performing filled a void in her, and gave her the love and adoration she couldn't get from her father, yet needed so badly.

Of course it wasn't long before she and Phillipe got married. They met after he came to see our show one night. That was such an incredible night. We were so on that night, it was amazing. The whole band just fed off the energy of the crowd, it was such a rush. Phillipe introduced himself after the show, and it was an instant attraction between those two. He was so handsome and obviously from a wealthy family. Charlotte fell for him right away. Though to be honest, she would always fall hard for whoever she dated. But then once the initial thrill went away, she would get bored and move on to the next man. That's why it was such a surprise to hear she and Phillipe were getting married. I never thought I'd see her settle down."

"Wow, this is amazing. I had no idea, and I'm sure no one else knew any of this. I wish she was still here. I would love to ask her about these stories. It would be so great if she was here with us," Emily stared down at her drink.

"Yes, I miss her terribly, even if the Charlotte I knew as a young girl was pretty much gone as she got older. Such a shame, really. I know what she was like when I talked to her, and I see what happened with the family. I know you didn't know her like I did. I wish you had, she was such a different person in those days," Kiki stared off in the distance before continuing.

"It wasn't just the way Thomas treated her that caused her mental downfall, as I prefer to think of it. There was much more that was much, much worse. It might help you understand her better, but you may need another drink before I tell you about that."

"I'm good. Actually I was going to get some coffee. Where are you staying, and how long will you be here?"

"I'm at the hotel in town, and I am not sure yet how long I'll stay. A lot depends on you guys. I'd like to meet the others, if that is possible. I know Jake and Jonathan don't live here, but I could try and see them later since I'm in the country."

"Of course you should meet Ellen and Graham! I know they

will be excited to meet you after all these years. We will definitely have to meet up with them."

Kiki smiled at Emily, "That will be great. I've so wanted to meet everyone. Well, I should say, again, since I did meet Jonathan, though of course he wouldn't remember me."

Emily looked quizzically at Kiki, "When was this? I don't remember Mom ever talking about you and Jonathan."

"I'm sure you know by now that your mother hid her pregnancy. Back in those days it was scandalous for a woman to have a baby out of wedlock. Nowadays, people give them baby showers and it's no big deal. It makes me mad at times what Charlotte went through, all because of what society thought back then. As I said, she was ahead of her time. However, as free spirited and rebellious as she was, she wasn't prepared to take on having an illegitimate baby, there is no telling what Thomas would have done. She hid her pregnancy and asked me to take care of the baby while she figured out her next step. I was living in Connecticut then, so I agreed. Charlotte went into labor, drove to Connecticut, had Jonathan and dropped him off with me. He was such an adorable baby. He lived with me for a year until she decided she would "adopt" him. After she came and got him, she told me that no one was to know any of this, and I was to have no contact with Jonathan. I was pretty upset as I had fallen in love with the little tyke, but she was adamant. That was when it really started to hit me that she wasn't the same girl I had known. As I'm sure you know, you couldn't argue with her. The funny thing is, after all she would say about Thomas, in a lot of ways, she turned out just like him. "

"Wow, we never knew who she left the kid with," Emily said.

"She would never talk about it, ever. Of course, we weren't exactly thrilled to get a new brother and things were pretty rough. She did some things I have not forgiven her for, all because of Jonathan. As much as I hate to say it, even though I love my mother, if it turns out he killed her she will have no one to blame but herself," Emily stared hard at Kiki, daring her to say something.

"I understand how you must feel. As I said earlier, I saw the change in Charlotte and it broke my heart. As close as we were, it didn't make it any easier to deal with her once she started losing her grip on reality," Kiki looked down at her drink, blinking back tears. Emily too, was crying.

"I'm sorry, I know how hateful that sounded, but all of us, except Jonathan, feel the same way. We loved her, and wanted her to love us, but it was never enough. From what you said about Grandfather, it seems she did turn into him. I don't have a lot of memories of him, but he always seemed glad to see us and treated us ok," Emily wiped her eyes, blinked back the tears and tried to compose herself. "It was just so damn frustrating dealing with her. Sometimes I think about the good things, but mostly what I remember are the bad times. It sucks. I feel like we got beat out of our childhood. Everyone thought we were living this fabulous life, and although it wasn't all bad, it wasn't fabulous by any means. I see pictures of us, and it looks like we were smiling and having fun, but I don't remember that. It all seems like it was a different family in those photos. Graham and Jake might remember it differently, since they were older, I don't know. It all just seems so sad."

Kiki took Emily's hands again. "I know, believe me, I know.

Charlotte loved you kids, although I know she didn't show it. I saw how Jonathan changed things. I often felt that maybe if she had been upfront about her pregnancy, and brought him home right away instead of waiting, maybe it would have turned out better. I think that was very hard on her. Even though she knew I was taking good care of him, I knew she felt horribly guilty about it, like she abandoned him. That's why she catered to his every whim and spoiled him like she did. Was it fair to the rest of you? Of course not. But unfortunately, that is the way she was. Maybe if she hadn't had such a screwed up time herself, but who knows."

Emily wiped her eyes again, and took a sip of coffee. "Ok, you keep saying about how screwed up her life was, what happened that was so horrible it mad her so crazy?"

Kiki took a breath and let it out slowly. "Have you ever met Charles?"

"Uncle Charles? Maybe when we were little, I don't even remember. Mom didn't talk a whole lot about him. I think the last mention of him was Grandfather's funeral. We were pretty young, and maybe it was because it was a sad occasion, but I remember it being a very stressful, tense affair. I can't remember if Uncle Charles came to the house. We weren't at the funeral itself, since we were so young, but I remember mom was in quite a state. You couldn't say anything to her, she bit your head off, and so we tried to stay out of the way."

"There were those that felt Charlotte was responsible for her dad's death, since she was there and they had a major blow up over Jonathan. People that worked in the house at the time remember hearing some of it, it seemed to revolve around the kid, and then she stormed out. When one of the help checked on

Thomas, he was dead on the floor from an apparent heart attack. I know Charlotte also blamed herself. If she didn't have Jonathan, her father wouldn't have gotten so upset. They wouldn't have fought, and he wouldn't have died. There may be some truth to that, but you can't change what happened. Thomas never would have accepted Jonathan, and Charlotte was a mother bear with her children, but especially that one, since he wasn't accepted by her family."

"Do you know who Jonathan's father is? Mom never told us."

"Yes. His name was Miguel and he was a polo player for your grandfather. He was incredibly handsome, of course, and at the time, one of the best polo players around. He was also quite a ladies man. I tried to warn your mother about him, but once she set her sights on someone, there was no stopping her. She used all of her charm to get him. It wasn't a very long affair, once she found out she was pregnant, he dropped her like a hot potato. From what she told me, he wanted her to have an abortion, which wasn't even legal here at the time. She tried to get him to accept Jonathan after he was born, but Miguel wanted no part of it. It wasn't long before he moved to England to play and she lost touch with him. Not that he had any intention of being a father, though he did get married. I remember how mad she was, and how hurt. It was just another rejection by another man."

Kiki took another sip of her drink and continued. "Anyway, this is the hard part. We were talking about Charles. He was your mother's half-brother. His mother died giving birth to him, and Thomas remarried pretty quickly to have a mother for the baby. I think he loved his new wife, though it's hard to say. Charles was groomed to be the perfect little man, his destiny was to take over the family business when Thomas retired, or died. Charlotte was born four years later and was spoiled rotten by her mother, who always wanted a little girl. Charles also loved Charlotte, and they were inseparable for years. Charlotte told me she was so lonely and lost after Charles started school and she was left alone in that great, big house with just her mother and the help. It wasn't all bad though, she had the ponies and later horses that she rode. She grew up showing and fox hunting. Anything she wanted, she was given."

Emily smiled, "Mom and I used to ride together when we went to Grandfather's place. I also showed my horse, and mom was always there to support me." Emily's smile faded somewhat, "at least until Jonathan started taking all her attention. He could be such a prick. Talk about spoiled and manipulative."

"I can see there isn't exactly any love lost between you two."

"No, there isn't. I don't think anyone in the family likes him, either. He's done too many things to all of us, let alone how he treated mom. Don't get me started on him, please continue what you were saying."

"Ok, Charles was sent to boarding school, as one would expect. Charlotte was miserable since she adored her older brother and now he wasn't close by, she missed him terribly. Eventually Charlotte started school herself. That's when it all changed, the summer of her twelfth year," Kiki sighed. "That year started her descent into madness, though I believe it would still have happened eventually. What happened that summer just triggered it. There were rumors she was sent overseas to get away from a married man, but that wasn't true. She was still an innocent child

131

at that time, and far too naive. What happened wasn't her fault, and instead of helping her, they sent her off to Europe in shame."

"What in the world happened that was so awful?" Emily wondered.

20 CHAPTER TWENTY

Charlotte lay on her bed trying to read a book, but her mind kept wandering. It was hot, too hot for June, in her opinion, especially for nine o'clock in the morning. Even in shorts and sleeveless top, blond hair pulled back in a ponytail, she was still too hot.

Suddenly she heard the sound of a car coming up the drive, followed by the sound of a car door slamming. Jumping off the bed, she ran to the open window and looked out, watching as her brother strode up to the front door. Charlotte turned and raced out of her room, down the hall to the stairs, leaning over the balcony in time to see Charles enter the house. Racing down the stairs she threw herself in his arms. "Charles! You're finally home!" Charlotte kissed her brother and hugged him tightly. "Easy there sister!" Charles laughed as he hugged her back and swung her in a circle. "I guess you missed me as much as I missed you."

"It has been so dull around here, you have no idea."

Charles placed her gently on the ground. "Where is everyone? I told them I was coming home today. I thought for sure they would be here."

"Mom went to visit a sick friend, and father is at the office, where else?" Charlotte pouted. "He has more important things to do than

babysit me."

Charles took both of her hands in his and holding her at arm's length slowly appraised her, his eyes traveling up and down her body. "Well, it sure doesn't look like you need a babysitter to me. You really are growing up, aren't you? I'll bet you have to beat the boys off, pretty as you are. You really have blossomed into a young woman."

Charlotte blushed and gave Charles a shove, "Stop it, you're embarrassing me," she giggled. "Now stop looking at me like that and come on, I'll fix you a snack and you can tell me all about what you have been up to," she said, as she spun around and headed for the kitchen. Charles grinned and watched her legs as she walked away, then followed her into the kitchen and sat on the counter. They chatted for a while, Charles regaling her with stories of his adventures at school, she telling him about her not as exciting life at home and her school. As he ate the sandwich she made for him he asked about their parents.

"When are they coming back? Did they say?"

"Not until dinner," Charlotte poured some more water for herself and her brother. "I can't stand this heat. I think this summer is going to be awful," Picking up a magazine from the table, she started fanning herself.

"Well, why don't we go to the beach for a swim? Grab your suit and some towels. I'll pack us something to eat and drink."

"Great idea!" Charlotte ran off to get her things, while Charles found the picnic basket and started filling it up. When his sister ran back down the stairs, they loaded up his car and headed for the beach. Charlotte chattered excitedly and both were in a good mood when they got to the beach. It was fairly deserted, considering the heat, but they still headed to a more secluded area they went to when they were kids. It

was a favorite spot and they would spend hours telling stories, playing games and hand. "This is nice," he agreed, "the perfect way to spend a summer day." Suddenly, with a wicked grin, Charles pulled Charlotte towards him and quickly dunked her under the water. Charlotte popped up, sputtering.

"Hey! No fair!" She yelled before splashing him and turning to swim away. Charles laughed and followed, grabbing her around the waist as they reached shallower water. Standing up he pulled her out of the water.

"Don't do it," she warned, before he picked her up and heaved her into the waves. Charlotte screamed, and then popped out again, laughing, before Charles made another grab for her. "Stop!" she laughed as he once again picked her up and tossed her into the waves, laughing. After a few more times, Charlotte begged for mercy as Charles held her in his arms.

"Ok, I suppose I can let you off easy this time," he smiled at her. "Let's go back to the beach and have some lunch, shall we?"

"Sounds good to me," she said as he gently carried her out of the water, her arms around his neck, her head against his chest. Reaching the beach blanket, he gently set her down. Charlotte picked up a towel and started drying herself off while Charles set out the sandwiches and glasses. Reaching back into the picnic basket, he pulled out a bottle of wine. Charlotte stared, aghast.

"Charles! What is that, we can't drink wine, we're too young! Where did you get that? Father will kill us if he finds out!"

Charles laughed as he filled the two glasses, "Don't be such a worry wart, who's going to tell? We drink all the time at school, it's no big deal. Here, have a taste, you don't want to spoil our picnic, do you?"

"No, I don't want to spoil it, but I just don't think it's right."

"It's fine, you have to grow up sometime, don't you trust me?" he responded, taking a sip from his glass. "Come on, you're all grown up now, it's about time you had your first glass of wine."

Charlotte looked at her glass, then at her brother. "Are you sure this is ok?" she asked.

"Have I ever steered you wrong before? Go ahead, try it," He watched as she tentatively took a sip. "See, that wasn't so bad, was it? Try some crackers with the cheese and the wine, it's very good together," Charlotte drank some more wine and nibbled on the cheese and crackers.

"This is pretty good," she finally said. Charles smiled as he refilled their glasses. They talked easily, sharing stories and laughing, eating and drinking the wine. Charlotte was reaching for some crackers when she knocked over her nearly empty glass. "Oops!" she giggled as she tried to set her glass back upright, before exploding into laughter.

Charles was laughing, too as he watched her struggle. Affecting a Southern accent, he said "Why Miss Charlotte, I do believe you may be a bit tipsy. Allow me," He set her glass upright and poured a little more wine into it.

Also speaking with a Southern accent, Charlotte replied, "I beg your pardon sir, how dare you imply I am drunk. I'm just a little clumsy, that's all," Once again she burst into a fit of laughter.

Laughing, Charles moved over to sit next to his sister. Leaning in close to her face he said, "I do believe I smell wine on your breath." Giggling, Charlotte tried to lean back when she fell flat on her back, laughing uncontrollably once again. Charles stretched out next to her, on his side, and leaned in close to her face. "I definitely smell wine, and you are definitely drunk, young lady," Suddenly, his mouth was on hers as he rolled on top of her. Charlotte's eyes got wide as she struggled to get up. Pushing against his chest, she managed to turn her face to the side.

"Stop it, what are you doing?" she cried.

Charles looked down at her, not moving off her body. "You've had your first taste of wine, now I think it's time you learned about men. I see the way they look at you, I see the way you flirt with them. You are still a virgin, aren't you?"

Charlotte was shocked, "Yes, of course I am! What are you talking about, we shouldn't be doing this, you're my brother, it isn't right!" she continued to try to push him off, but Charles just laughed.

"Half-brother, and it's ok, no one will know. I think it's better if you learn from someone that loves you, and cares about you, don't you agree?" he said before kissing her again. Pinning her body down with his, he reached for her bathing suit and tugged at it, pulling the top down to her waist. Charlotte continued to struggle until he grabbed her wrists and held her arms down on the ground above her head. "Now listen, this will be a lot easier if you just go along with it. I'm not going to hurt you, so just lie still and behave," With one hand holding both of hers above her head, he peeled her bathing suit off her body, letting out another low whistle. "You are so damn beautiful," he said as he started kissing her breasts.

"Charles, please, stop, I don't want to do this," Charlotte sobbed. "Please stop."

"Listen to me, you are going to like this, so stop crying. Just lie there and do as I tell you," Grabbing her glass of wine, he poured it over her breasts, and then proceeded to lick and suck them, his tongue twirling around her nipples. Despite herself, Charlotte started to feel

herself respond to his tongue. "See, now we're getting somewhere," he murmured against her skin. Still holding her arms above her head, he slipped one knee between her legs and pushed them apart. Quickly, he pulled his bathing suit off, his erection huge. Charlotte screamed as he entered her, but he quickly covered her mouth again with his and he began thrusting into her, his pace quickening until with one final thrust his whole body shuddered and he collapsed on her.

Charlotte lay sobbing beneath him. "Why did you do that, it did hurt, why?" she cried.

Raising himself off her chest, he caressed her face with his hand, finally letting her arms down. "The first time is always like that, don't worry, next time it won't be so bad. You need to know how to please a man," Staring at her body, he once again began caressing her breasts, before moving his hands between her legs. Once again she tried to struggle, grabbing his hand and trying to pull away. Charles just laughed and once again grabbed her hands and held them above her head. "What did I tell you? Now be a good girl and learn your lessons. We have all afternoon to get this right," Feeling himself get hard, he once again penetrated her. "Let's try this again," He said as he began a slow, rhythmic, thrust. Charlotte, lay still, sobbing. "Remember, I'm doing this because I love you," he said before once again closing his mouth over hers.

As he got dressed, Charles looked down at Charlotte. She had curled up on her side in a fetal position, sobbing quietly. "Hey, get up and get dressed, we need to go home," He started packing up the picnic, throwing the empty wine bottle into the bushes. "Come on, stop crying and let's go. We don't want to be late."

Charlotte turned her tear stained face to him, "I feel sick, I think I'm going to throw up," Suddenly she got to her feet and staggered to the bushes, violently vomiting.

"Oh gross. Here, have some cola, it will help. You're going to have a hangover tomorrow," Charles handed her a bottle of cola. Charlotte wiped her mouth on a towel and sat back down, gingerly accepting the drink.

Glaring at Charles she said, "What are mother and father going to say when they hear about this?" Charles spun around and angrily grabbed her by the shoulders.

"What do you mean, what are they going to say? About what? How you got drunk on wine and came on to me? You are not saying a word about this, do you hear me? I'll deny anything ever happened, except maybe you getting drunk. Who do you think they will believe, anyway, huh? You? Not likely. You are going to go home, and not say a word. If anyone asks, you are sick with the flu. Do you hear me?"

"They'll have to believe me! You can't get away with this, it's wrong! I trusted you! I loved you, how could you do this to me?" Charlotte sobbed.

Smiling, Charles stroked her hair and responded, "I told you it was because I love you, remember? You didn't really want some guy who doesn't love you getting to you first. And no one will believe you, so I'm telling you for the last time, you will not speak of this. Ever. Do you hear me? Now, clean yourself up and let's get going."

"I hate you, I don't ever want to see you again, ever!" she yelled as she stumbled along, following her brother to the car.

Neither spoke as they drove back to the house. As they pulled up the driveway, they noticed their parent's cars parked there. Charles looked over at his sister and smiled. "Remember what I said, this is between us.

It's our secret," He put a hand on her shoulder. "Are you ready?"

Shrugging his hand off his shoulder, Charlotte replied, "Don't touch me, don't you ever touch me again," before opening the car door and walking unsteadily to the front door. Just as she reached the door, it opened and her mother was standing there.

"Charlotte, are you okay? You look terrible. Come on inside, what's wrong? Charles, darling, you too, come on in," ushering the two of them inside, she put her arm around Charlotte. "Honey what on earth is wrong?"

"She's just feeling a bit ill, I think she might be coming down with something. Isn't that right sis?" Charles glanced at Charlotte, who glared at her brother.

"Yes, I really think I need to lie down, please excuse me mother," she replied dully as she stumbled her way up the stairs to her bedroom. Falling face down on her bed, the room spinning around her, she eventually cried herself to sleep.

21 CHAPTER TWENTY-ONE

Tears ran down Emily's face as she listened to Kiki. "How horrible! We had no idea she had gone through anything like that, she never said a word."

"You have to remember, back then there were no advocacy groups, no incest survivors groups, none of that. She had no one to talk to, no one who would listen to her and get her the help she needed. Not to mention what should have happened to Charles. Nowadays, he would be thrown in jail and labeled a sex offender. Well, maybe, he is rich so it might still be pushed under the rug. The rich really are different, and this certainly isn't anything new. Incest happens in a lot more families than you realize, especially wealthy ones. As well as, theft, embezzlement, adultery, drugs, alcoholism, physical abuse and even murder. The difference is, it is either hidden away, or if it is exposed, they have the money to buy the best lawyers and get away with it. Look at all the celebrities and politicians involved in scandals, nothing happens to them. And those are just the ones you hear about, trust me, there are tons of stuff that no one ever finds out about. So, your poor mother was screwed, no pun intended."

"How did she handle it? I'm sure she still had to deal with him. He was her brother after all. Her parents didn't notice anything wrong? Not even her mother?"

"Parents see what they want to see. I'm sure her mother suspected something was wrong, but Charlotte wasn't about to try and tell them what happened. She knew he was right when he said no one would believe her, especially Thomas. Her mother would go along with whatever Thomas said. She wouldn't have fought for her child, not like women today. Charlotte tried to avoid Charles, but unfortunately, the abuse continued all summer while he was home from school. I don't know for sure why she was sent to Europe, my guess is her change in attitude. Not having anyone to talk to about what was happening to her, she shut herself off from everyone. I also believe there may have been a suicide attempt and after that her parents figured the best way to handle her was to ship her off to school. She was becoming a liability to the family name and there was no way Thomas would tolerate that. So, off she went. In hindsight, maybe it did her some good, at least it got her away from Charles, and she was finally able to come into her own after we became friends and started the band."

Emily felt sick as she listened to Kiki. "You said you met in school?"

Kiki smiled, "Yes. She was this withdrawn little beauty, and I was this outgoing rebel. There was something about her that drew me to her that first day. She looked so frail and lost, I don't know, maybe I felt the need to try to take care of her. Or maybe because I felt like we were misfits and we should be friends. I honestly don't remember. We hit it off and she slowly started coming out of her shell. We ended up rooming together, too. I tell you what, your mother had a wicked sense of humor and adventure once she opened up. She obviously had some major trust issues, but once she realized she could trust me, man oh man, the pranks we would pull. Anything to break the boredom, she was a lot of fun in those days."

"How did you find out about Charles, did she tell you?"

"Not right away. I mean, that wasn't something you talked about, there was a lot of shame involved. It was at least a year or so, it may have even been while we were in the band before I found out. I started to notice something wasn't right when he came to visit. We had been there almost a year when he showed up. He had been writing her, though she didn't tell me about that until much later on. I guess when she didn't respond to his postcards, he decided to visit. Apparently she wasn't really writing anyone back that often and they became concerned. There was no cell phone, no texting, and no Internet back then. Sometimes you would get a phone call, but it was very expensive and the connections were not always very good, so everyone wrote letters, or sent postcards, that's how people communicated in those days. Charles offered to check up on her during his break from school. He was so handsome. I remember we were walking back from class or something, and he was standing at the front door of the school. Charlotte immediately stopped, and got very pale and quiet. It was like the first time I saw her, she just closed up again. I was going to leave them alone, but she told me to stay, so I did. She told him she was fine, they talked a bit, and then we went to our room. Men were not allowed inside the dorms, and he ended up leaving. When we got to the room, she was shaking and I asked if she was ok, she said she was and didn't want to talk about it. All of us had some issue or other with families, there were quite a few skeletons in closets back then, so I didn't press the issue. Anyway, since she seemed better the next day, I pretty much wrote it off. "

Emily was silent, letting what Kiki told her sink in, "I still can't wrap my head around this. How did you find out?"

Kiki thought a moment then replied, "I think I was more suspicious that summer, the first year we were there. Usually, everyone goes home for the summer, and there was a lot of excitement about going home. Except for Charlotte. The closer it got to school letting out, the quieter she got. She never said out right that she didn't want to go home, but it was pretty obvious. I finally asked her about it and she told me she didn't want to go. I asked if she wanted to come home with me. I knew my parents would probably be glad I had a friend to keep me busy. My parents weren't that much different from hers, maybe that's another reason we hit it off so well. Anyway, she jumped at the chance to stay with me, so that's what we did. We had a blast that summer, too. Charles tried to visit, but we managed to avoid him, other than one weekend where we did go to her family's house to see her mom. Fortunately, Charles was away that weekend, and she was able to be a little more like herself. Even so, there was a definite change in her when she was around her family, it was so sad. Clearly, there was an issue, even as young as I was, I could see it."

"I guess that explains why she would take us to Grandfather's place when he wasn't around. Even when we were together, she was always very uptight and wanted to leave as soon as possible," Emily looked down, slowly shook her head from side to side.

"I'm not surprised. I met Thomas and he scared the daylights out of me, he was so stern. I can understand why Charlotte felt so isolated once she no longer had Charles to hang out with. Anyway, every year it was the same thing, she would stay with us on holidays, only seeing her mom on occasion. I did like her mom. It really was a shame she couldn't get through to Charlotte, but she was not a strong person and there was no way she could stand up to Thomas, or Charles for that matter. I know she loved her daughter, but she had a tough time showing it. She would write all the time, and send money, but Charlotte rarely wrote back." Kiki took another sip of her drink. "You asked how I found out. I think it was when we were about 16 or 17. Your mother never drank, ever. Especially not wine, which was really an oddity when we were in France. I mean, everyone drinks wine in France! She wouldn't touch it. After I heard what happened, I figured it was all about control, she wasn't going to lose control like that ever again. I had started drinking, and we both were smoking. Even though she wouldn't drink, we had discovered pot, which she had no qualms about. It calmed her without her feeling like she was losing control. You should have seen your mother stoned," Kiki laughed, "she was hysterical. So one day, we were in our room, I had a couple of beers, we were both smoking and getting a bit of a buzz on the pot and I think I asked her about what she had against wine. I guess she trusted me enough by then, or it was the dope, but she started talking and told me the whole story. I was quite shocked, as you can imagine, but I think it helped her to tell someone, especially someone that believed her. It explained the way she was around boys, too. She wasn't dating yet, and pretty much ignored all the boys our age. But she was very flirtatious with older men. I think that was also a control type issue. "

Emily was thoughtful, "I'm glad you were there for her, the poor thing. It's still hard to believe we are talking about my mother, it's like I'm hearing about a stranger. Mom was always so secretive about her childhood and life before she married dad, now I know why. It does explain a lot. Tell me about Phillipe, she didn't kill him did she?"

Kiki smiled sadly, "No, she didn't. As I mentioned earlier, Phillipe and Charlotte started dating after he came to hear us play. They were planning to get married when Charlotte was called home because her mother was dying. Charlotte hurried back to the states, but got there too late, her mother had died literally moments after she got to the house. Charlotte was devastated of course, she felt guilty for not getting there in time. I'm sure Thomas didn't help her, either. He would have blamed her in some way if he could. From what I remember, he wanted her to stay in the states and pretty much take over as lady of the house, but she told him she was getting married. There was a bit of a battle, Thomas would not accept her eloping after all, and Charlotte and Phillipe ended up having the proper wedding Thomas wanted. I was her maid of honor, and Victor was the best man. Charles wasn't there. I don't remember the excuse for him not being there. She hadn't told Phillipe what happened and had no intention of telling him. She just wanted to get married and head back to England, where we were all living at the time. Anyway, the wedding went off nice and proper, and the newlyweds headed off for their honeymoon. Phillipe's family had a yacht of course, and they sailed off to Greece. She was so happy for a change, after they came back she set up house and we'd get together all the time. I think she was the happiest I had ever seen her. Phillipe doted on her, and spoiled her rotten. It was the first time she ever had a man that showed he truly cared about her, and she blossomed while she was with him. We even talked about putting the band back together. Phillipe was all for it, after all that is how they met. Now that she was a married woman, Thomas didn't have quite the same control over her. He used to use his money to keep her in line, threaten to cut her off and all that. But she married into a wealthy family, and it wasn't such a big deal anymore. For the first time she could do what she wanted without having to worry about worrying about being a disgrace to the family.

They were married about a year or so when Charles showed up. They were going sailing again, and somehow Charles ended up getting invited. I think Charlotte felt that she was safe now that she was older and married, surely he wouldn't try anything. I wasn't there. I only know what she told me later. Apparently Charles hadn't gotten over his obsession with her, and after he had a few drinks, tried to take up where he left off. Charlotte fought him off, but Phillipe walked in on them and went ballistic. He and Charles got into a huge fight, and ultimately, Charles ended up knocking Phillipe out and pushed him overboard. There were some other people on board who heard the commotion and came to help, but it was too late. By the time they were able to stop the boat, and send a lifeboat out to him, he was dead. Of course the whole thing was hushed up, the story was he was drunk and fell overboard, though of course others thought Charlotte was the one that pushed him. Once again, even though she tried to say it was Charles, no one believed her. The police believed Charles, who was putting the blame on her, saying she was drunk and got into the fight and was responsible. He was such a bastard. Thomas closed ranks and paid off whoever he needed to make it all go away, and brought her home under a cloud of suspicion and scandal. I wrote her every day, but it was months before she wrote back. I was frantic with worry, and when I finally got her letters, I could tell things had changed, she just wasn't the same," Kiki looked sadly at Emily. "I think that was when she really changed, it was like she accepted that men would always betray her, there was no getting away from it."

"What about Charles, he didn't molest her anymore, did he? And Dad, I thought he rescued her from her family."

"Charles didn't touch her after that, I think by now she was old enough that he finally left her alone. Not to mention he did kill her husband, even if no one would listen to her then. Your father showed up one day to pay his respects and check on her. I'm sure you know Victor and Phillipe had been best friends, and he was always attracted to her. They started dating and after it got serious, Thomas tried to break them up. Your father saw the way she was being treated, knew how she was when she was with Phillipe, and decided he was going to save her by marrying her and taking her away from her family. Thomas of course was against it, but Victor was pretty strong willed and determined to save her. Unfortunately for Victor, I think it was already too late. They had a small wedding, no big wedding after all the scandal of her first marriage, and well, you know the rest."

Emily was outraged, "What the hell! How can he get away with murdering her husband?! I can't believe it, and then to blame her like that? That is outrageous! Couldn't anything be done?"

"I know, believe me, I was furious, too, but there was no proof of anything other than there had been drinking, they had been smoking dope, a fight happened, and he went overboard. It

148

was her word against Charles. And who do you think they will believe? Especially since Thomas would never believe anything bad against his son. Period. So she got screwed, again."

"What about Dad, did he know the whole story? I can't believe he didn't stick up for her."

Kiki shook her head, "She never told him. I think he suspected she didn't do it. Your dad was pretty sharp, but she never told him about the abuse, or what really happened. I think by now she didn't trust anyone and just kept it to herself. After they had been married awhile, her mental state started getting worse. I think he probably believed what Thomas told him. I know he and Thomas became allies after the divorce when he was trying to get custody of all of you. It was so sad, as I'm sure you know, you lived it. Once she got pregnant she went downhill in a hurry."

Emily smiled sadly at Kiki, "The little I've gotten to know you today, it's a shame mom didn't let you keep Jonathan. I feel like he would have turned out completely different. Maybe she wouldn't have felt so guilty about him that she would have treated us normally. Or at least if she had been honest enough to admit she was pregnant, and had the baby without dumping him on you. What she did wasn't fair to you or any of us. I would feel sorry for Jonathan, but she gave him everything his whole life, and I think he got what he deserved when he married Kelly."

"Thank you Emily, as I said, I was heartbroken when I had to give Jonathan up. I'd like to think he would be a rock and roller if he stayed with me. I could see him fronting a band, maybe I would even have been in it, too. That would have been something to see," Kiki laughed, "Tell me about Jonathan and Kelly."

Emily picked at her salad. "Jonathan and Kelly, the golden couple. They are two of the biggest assholes that ever walked the face of the earth. They are perfectly suited for each other, so I guess it was destiny they hooked up. They met in school, I really didn't pay much attention at first. Jonathan was so good looking, he always had women throwing themselves at him. I couldn't keep up with all of his girlfriends. At the time, I was working at the bar that I ended up buying, so it wasn't like I was paying much attention. Mom used to talk about Kelly, obviously she was more involved with them than I was, but she thought Kelly was perfect. I didn't even meet her until their wedding, and I must say, she was gorgeous. They were so good looking, they both looked like models. When you saw them together, you couldn't look at anything else. I tried to like her, considering I still was okay with Jonathan. He hadn't become quite the master manipulator yet, but there was something phony about her from the start. It was funny when Graham and Stella showed up. I could tell it took Stella about five minutes tops to size her up, and that was it I could tell she couldn't stand her. Stella is good that way. She has a way of seeing through bullshit to what people are really like. Ellen liked her, of course, she always tries to like and please everyone. Plus, Ellen would do whatever it took to stay on mom's good side. She doesn't do well with conflict and drama. It's why she ended up moving to Australia for a while."

"Oh? I didn't realize she had lived there."

"It was only for a few years. It was while she lived there that I met my roommate Gail. I was visiting Ellen and we met at a dance bar. Gail ended up moving here, my previous roommate had just moved out, Gail needed a place to stay, and I needed a roommate. It all worked out pretty well. Eventually, she and I bought the bar, and though it's been a struggle at times, it's all worth it."

Kiki smiled mischievously, "Do you have live music and need a beyond middle age rocker chick for entertainment? I could put together another band."

Emily choked on her drink, laughing, "That would be really cool! Don't joke with me about it, I'll take you seriously and then you will be on the stage. It might be really fun!"

Kiki laughed, "Well, you just never know. Look at all these groups that are still out there playing, when other people that age are in retirement homes. Yeah, you know, we'll have to talk about this."

Emily smiled broadly, "You got it. I can hardly wait. Wait until I tell Gail about this, she will love it," Emily paused for a moment before continuing, "Anyway, back to Jonathan and Kelly. Let me tell you about those two."

22 CHAPTER TWENTY-TWO

He stood at the edge of the clearing in the woods, staring at her. His eyes bored into hers, before slowly traveling down her body, pausing on her heaving breasts. She trembled under his stare, her knees quivered, her legs gave out and she fell crashing to the ground. In an instant he was at her side, picking her up and holding her against his chest. His lips met hers, crushing…

"Kiki, what are you doing?"

"Agh!" Kiki jumped and struggled out from under the blankets on the bed, her heart pounding. "Charlotte! You scared the crap out of me! What are you doing sneaking up on me like that?!"

"I'm sneaking up? I'm not the one hiding under the blankets, what are you hiding under there?" Charlotte reached out and quickly grabbed the book Kiki was reading, "'Damsels in Distress'? Where did you get this? Are you crazy? Do you know what they will do to us if they find this trash in our room? We'll be thrown out of school! And is that a beer? What are you doing?" Charlotte whispered loudly.

Kiki grabbed the book back from her friend, "Shhh, keep it down! No one will know if you don't say anything. Besides, it's not trash, it's romance. You should read it, it's exciting, and romantic, and.."

"And trash," Charlotte cut her off. "I can't believe you would jeopardize our education for this, this, this, book. And the beer. What am I going to do with you?"

"You can start by turning off the light and let me finish reading my book." Kiki crawled back under the covers and turned her flashlight on.

"Oh, that's great. Like no one will know you're reading, and I'm sure they will think you are studying for your biology test tomorrow."

Kiki's response was muffled, "I AM studying biology," she replied before breaking out in giggles.

Charlotte rolled her eyes. "You're reading a dirty book."

"It's romance."

"No it's not."

"Yes, it is, in fact, maybe you should read it before you pass judgment. Come here, just read a little."

"No, absolutely not! I am not reading that trash, and you need to get rid of it before we get kicked out. I get enough grief from my father about the band. Do you know what would happen to me if I get kicked out of school over some trashy book?" Charlotte moved over to stand over Kiki under the covers.

"Will you give it a rest, and keep your voice down. Don't worry, if we get kicked out, we still have the band. It's not like we'll starve. We may even make it big and be rich. Then you won't have to worry about your father's opinions."

Charlotte watched for a few seconds before pulling the cover off Kiki.

"Right, that's easy for you to say, you don't know my father."

"Will you stop? Let me read, already," Kiki was absorbed in her book. Charlotte casually leaned over and read over Kiki's shoulder.

"What the..? Oh my," Charlotte said. Slowly, and without missing a beat, she lowered herself on the bed next to Kiki.

"Don't turn the page yet, you know I can't read as fast as you," she told Kiki, who just laughed.

"Told you it wasn't a bad book, it's romantic," Kiki sighed as they continued reading into the night.

It was early afternoon as Kiki and Charlotte helped drag the equipment out of the car. The band had acquired a used, early sixties London Taxi cab to transport them and the equipment to the shows. It was a tight fit, but they were also on a tight budget. Whatever didn't fit came along in whatever other vehicle they could scrounge up. As Charlotte helped Gary set up his drum set, Kiki and Mick, who played lead guitar, and David, who played bass, headed back to the car. Kiki and David had been dating for several months and he took her hand as they headed back. Once all the equipment was unloaded and carried into the pub for the show later that evening, David and Mick asked Kiki if she wanted to go for a ride to view a very scenic area outside the town.

"Sure, let me just tell Charlotte so she doesn't worry about where I am," Kiki agreed. After letting Charlotte know where she was going, Kiki hopped into the back of the cab with David, and with Mick at the wheel,

they drove out of town, down a quiet country road before finally turning down another deserted road. The road ran between some forests, huge trees on either side of the car darkened the sky. At last they found the place they had been looking for. It was a clearing in the forest, overlooking a beautiful river. They got out of the car and looked out over the river.

"This is so beautiful," Kiki sighed as she gazed out over the water.

"A beautiful sight for a beautiful woman," David smiled down at her. At almost 6 feet, slim, with long, brown hair and dark eyes, he made Kiki's heart flutter just looking at him. "What do you say we get back in the car for a bit, we have plenty of time before the show starts to have some fun," David's eyes glittered as he smiled.

Kiki's heart started hammering in her chest. "Sure," she replied as they headed back to the car with Mick trailing behind them. David and Kiki got in the huge backseat and started kissing. David held her face in his hands, gently caressing her before running his hands through her hair. Kiki was also doing the same to David when she felt his hands on her breasts. It took her a moment to realize it was Mick's, not David's, hands she was feeling. Startled, she pulled away from David, wondering what he would do about it.

"Is it ok luv?" David asked her.

Kiki thought for a few seconds before answering, "Uh, sure, it's ok." With that Mick started kissing the back and sides of her neck, while David kissed her lips, moving his tongue down her throat. Kiki moaned as Mick's hands caressed her breasts, while she worked at the buttons on David's shirt, finally pulling it off and reaching for his belt. Mick yanked Kiki's shirt off her head and undid her bra, tossing it to the front of the car. As Kiki undid David's pants, he moved his mouth to her freed breasts, licking and sucking first one nipple, then the other. She felt Mick take off his shirt and he turned her face to his, kissing her deeply on the mouth. Kiki groaned with pleasure as she felt someone, she didn't even know who, shove her skirt up and pull off her panties. She felt herself being pushed gently but firmly onto her back as fingers explored between her legs. Moving her hips to the rhythm, she quickly climaxed, bucking her hips up. She was still climaxing when David grabbed her by the hips and thrust his penis into her, pounding along with her orgasm. At the same time, Mick, fully erect, put his penis in her face. Kiki grabbed it with her hand and took him in her mouth, tongue swirling around the head of his penis. Mick groaned and thrusting faster, he and David both climaxed at the same time. Kiki also started another orgasm as she swallowed and sucked harder on Mick's erection.

The three of them collapsed for a moment, before David and Mick switched places. This time Mick lifted her hips to his face, and started licking between her legs, teeth gently pulling on her skin as he nibbled on her. Kiki moaned, and thrust her hips again as this time David put his erection in her mouth, hands kneading her breasts. Sucking wildly, Kiki then felt as Mick entered her. Her hands reached around David's ass and pulled him deeper into her mouth, as Mick pounded between her legs. She felt the warm semen in her throat as David climaxed. She was so close herself, but as David removed himself, Mick suddenly turned her over onto her stomach, riding her from behind as his hands kneaded her ass. Kiki screamed as she started coming, Mick coming a few seconds later.

As the three lay naked, sweating and exhausted, Kiki smiled dreamily at both of them. "Oh my God, that was amazing," she said.

"Yes it was," Mick replied. "David is one lucky guy to have someone like you," his hand softly squeezing one of her breasts. "Anytime you want to do this again, just say the word," he smiled at *her, and then kissed her on the lips.*

"I think that can be arranged, as long as David is ok with it," Kiki looked questioningly over at David.

"I'm sure that won't be a problem," he laughed as he leaned over and kissed her, too. "I wish we had more time now, but if we expect to get to the show on time, we had better get going," Both men looked longingly at Kiki, but she sighed and sat up, gathering up her clothes.

"I guess you're right. But man, that was something," she smiled dreamily as she and the others got dressed.

Charlotte was pacing outside the club when Kiki and the others returned. "Where have you been? I have been looking everywhere for you! Do you realize we go on in twenty minutes?" she yelled at them. "I didn't know what I was going to do if you didn't get back in time!"

Kiki stopped as David and Mick, grinning sheepishly, continued into the club.

"Well, we're back now and we have plenty of time, so calm down," Kiki started towards the door, Charlotte following.

"Where did you go?" Charlotte persisted.

"We went for a drive, now let it go, will you? As you were saying, we have a show to do. We can talk about it later," Kiki and Charlotte joined the rest of the band, who were warming up backstage.

"Well, we all ready then?" David asked the girls. "Let's do this."

Phillipe nursed his drink along as he watched the band. He was impressed with how good they were, but found he couldn't take his eyes off the blond singer. Not that the dark haired one wasn't a beauty, but there was something about the blond he found mesmerizing. He wondered if she had a boyfriend, she looked too young to be married. As they started the next number, he found the blond staring at him as she sang, as if he was the only one in the club and she was singing just for him. Her voice was so amazing he found he was losing himself in the song, and was startled at the end when the place erupted in applause. As the band took their bows, he was on his feet and heading backstage, determined to meet this bewitching creature.

Charlotte and Kiki were still soaring as they raced backstage, mostly from the show, but also helped along with the joint they had shared before they had stepped onstage.

"That was so amazing! That had to be one of our best shows ever!" Kiki shouted. "Charlotte, what was with you and that guy in the front row? You two seemed so totally in tune, it gave me chills to watch."

"I don't know what came over me, I think it was just the song. And he was sitting there watching me so intently, I just forgot where I was," Charlotte blushed as the others laughed.

"Well, don't be embarrassed, that was so cool," Kiki said as she turned and noticed Phillipe heading towards them. "Speak of the devil. It does appear you have an admirer."

Charlotte looked up as Phillipe reached them. Phillipe was tall, well built, good looking with dark brown hair and dark, intense eyes.

Taking her hand in his, he brought it to his lips as with a soft French accent, he introduced himself, "Bonjour, Mademoiselle, my name is Phillipe Charbaneau. Allow me to say you are the most beautiful and *talented singer I have ever had the pleasure of meeting."*

Charlotte blushed again, "Thank you sir, that is too kind. My name is Charlotte. These are my friends Kiki, David, Mick and Billy." After introductions were made, Phillipe turned again to Charlotte.

"If it would be ok, I'd like you to join me for dinner," he said as he gazed steadily into her eyes. Feeling her knees going weak, she found she could barely speak.

"That would be nice," she replied softly as Kiki, who was standing behind Phillipe, grinned broadly. "Let me get cleaned up a bit, I'll be right back." Charlotte backed up a step, almost tripping over Mick, who was standing behind her.

Phillipe smiled, "Of course, I will be waiting at my table." Kissing her hand once again before he released it, Philippe turned, and headed back into the club.

"Holy crap!" cried Kiki, grabbing Charlotte's arm and dragging her to the restroom "Come on, let's get you freshened up and on your date!"

In the restroom, Charlotte started to panic. "What am I doing? I don't even know him? Please don't leave me alone!"

Kiki was brushing her friend's hair, and looked at her in the mirror. "Are you nuts? That guy is so gorgeous! And he has money, look at how he was dressed, and the way he speaks. This one could be the one, don't blow it!" Charlotte looked frightened as Kiki continued. "Look, I know what you have been through, and how hard it is for you to trust any man. But," she said as she gently turned Charlotte to face her, "what you need to remember is this. Don't let what happened to you ruin your life." Kiki held up a hand as Charlotte started to protest, "I see how you are on dates. I know you are afraid of sex, but honey, this is the nineteen sixties already! We are not our mothers, standing around all day in the kitchen with our aprons on waiting on our men to come home. We can be and do what we want, we can have sex without feeling guilty! Plus," she continued as Charlotte tried to turn away, "this is your way of getting back at Charles. Think of it. You are in control, not him. You can meet other men and have sex on your terms, not theirs. It puts the power back in your hands. You are free!" Kiki stared into her friend's eyes, "Please, do this. Let go of the past and take control over your life for a change. Forget about your father, you don't need him. Forget about Charles, he's in the past. Live your life for you, Charlotte."

Charlotte's eyes were tearing up as she listened to her best friend. Finally she nodded and threw her arms around Kiki, holding on tight.

Thank you Kiki, you are the best friend I could ever ask for! I'm still not sure I can do this, but I'll try. I promise I'll try," Holding Kiki at arm's length, Charlotte glanced in the mirror before turning back to Kiki. "Do I look alright?"

Kiki smiled, "You look amazing. Now, go have some fun for a change! And, I want all the details when you get home tonight!" Laughing she turned Charlotte to face the door and gave her a gentle push. "Now go!"

Phillipe sucked in his breath and held it, as he saw Charlotte coming towards him. She was like a vision. She seemed to float across the floor, long blond hair falling softly to her waist, her cobalt blue eyes wide, mouth in a tentative smile as she approached. Standing up he held out a chair for her to sit, as she reached the table.

"Thank you," she said as she sat down.

160

"My pleasure. I've ordered a bottle of wine, but if you'd like something else, please tell me."

"Oh, I'm sorry, I don't drink wine. Soda or water would be fine for me." Charlotte felt panic starting to rise. Taking a deep breath she tried to remember what Kiki told her, hoping to steady her nerves.

"That is no problem," Philippe said as he signaled the waiter. "Whatever your heart desires, you shall have." Gazing into her eyes again, Charlotte felt herself melting. She had never felt this way with a man before. Except Charles, she flushed as unbidden images of her half-brother rushed into her memory. Once, she had loved him with all her heart, which made what had happened all the more horrible. Charlotte was never able to totally forgive herself for what happened. Despite being a victim, she still blamed herself. After all, hadn't he told her it was her fault for the way she had dressed, and how she had gotten drunk and led him on? Shaking the images from her head, she once again looked at Phillipe and smiled.

"You looked so serious for a moment, is everything alright?" he asked, looking concerned.

"Yes, everything is wonderful," Charlotte smiled back as she let his voice float over and around her, wrapping her in comfort as he talked and told her about himself. She felt Kiki would be proud, as she hadn't bolted from the table yet. Charlotte had taken a few lovers after what happened with Charles, but none that touched her the way she was feeling now. She had never enjoyed sex after that day, but maybe Kiki was right. She wished she was more carefree like Kiki, maybe she was right. Maybe this is the one, maybe this time it would be different, time to take control of her life. Isn't that what Kiki said? She smiled again as she started to relax. Soon, she found herself talking about herself, how she and Kiki started the band, school, everything but Charles. That wasn't something *she was willing to share.*

They talked for hours, lingering over coffee after the waiter cleared their plates from their dinner. Phillipe had found it funny, and refreshing how much food Charlotte had put away. She giggled as she thought of the joint she had shared earlier. No wonder she was starving. Reluctantly, they finally had to leave, as the club was closing for the night. Phillipe escorted her to his car, and held the door as she got in. Settling in next to her, he asked where she lived and she gave him the address of the school. When they reached the school, he once again escorted her to the door, where he stopped. Men were not allowed in the school, so he took her hands and gently kissed them.

"I had a wonderful time," she said.

"Me too. I'd like to see you again. How about tomorrow afternoon? Perhaps have lunch?" Phillipe patiently waited for her response.

"That would be great," She agreed.

"I will see you tomorrow," he said as this time he learned forward and gently kissed her on the lips. "Until tomorrow." He smiled as he turned and walked back to the car.

"Until tomorrow," Charlotte whispered as she watched him go.

"Nothing? He didn't make a move at all?" Kiki couldn't believe her ears. "Wow."

"Nope, he was a perfect gentleman. We talked all night long. I could listen to that voice forever," Charlotte sighed. "We're having lunch today, too."

"Maybe he will make his move today," Kiki laughed. "Anyway, I'm glad you had a good time, it's nice to see you looking so happy and relaxed."

"Yeah, it was weird, there is just something about him that is so different from anyone else. I am really looking forward to seeing him again. Though I must admit, part of me is still waiting for the bad news, like he's really married or broke or something. Or, what will happen when he finds out about Charles? He'll probably never want to see me again," Charlotte worried as feeling of despair crept in. Breaking into tears, she cried, "All I want is someone to love me for me! Is that so wrong? Not because I'm rich, not because they want sex, but because they want me!" Kiki hugged her sobbing friend.

"Stop it! He is not married, or a cad, or broke, and he isn't going to leave you. I saw the way he looked at you! And besides, you don't have to tell him anything you don't want to tell him. And people do love you, I love you, the guys in the band love you. Phillipe will love you once he gets to know you. Stop worrying, you have a lunch date to prepare for."

Taking a deep breath, Charlotte replied, "You're right, it's just so hard to trust. I'm so scared of being hurt or taken advantage of again."

"You will be fine. You just need to believe in yourself," smiled Kiki.

Phillipe soon became a regular wherever the band was playing. He and Charlotte had been dating for a couple of weeks, when one night after dinner, as they settled into his car, Phillipe turned to her and asked, "Where do you like to wake up, the city or the country?" Her heart pounding in her chest, knees weak, she thought it was a good thing she was already sitting or she might collapse. After a beat she blushed and replied "The country."

Smiling broadly, Phillipe leaned over and gently kissed her lips, then starting the car, he said, "The country it is."

Charlotte tried to find out where they were going, but all he would tell her was that it was a surprise. Finally she gave up and just enjoyed watching the beautiful scenery fly by. Soon they were pulling into a long, tree lined drive that eventually opened up to a large estate. The drive turned into a circular driveway, now lined on the inside of the circle with well- trimmed hedges. The house was a huge, stone structure. The main part was three stories, with a one story wing on either side. The lawn was well manicured and seemed to go on forever, before meeting up with the woods on one side. The other side was all gently rolling grass as far as she could see. On the right, next to the house, was the carriage house and stable. Several huge trees surrounded the house and drive, shading it from the sun. Even though Charlotte had been raised in mansions and was used to living on estates, she was still blown away by the beauty.

Climbing from the car, she slowly turned, taking in the view. "This place is gorgeous, who lives here?" she asked.

"I do. At least when I'm not staying at my apartment in the city," Taking her hand, Phillipe led her up the wide front stairs and they entered the house. Charlotte found herself in a grand hallway, with a wide, winding, open stairway leading to the upper floors. There was a door to the right leading to the parlor, another door on the left opened to the dining room, and further back on the left a door opened to the kitchen, and presumably, one of the wings. On the right was another door leading to the other wing.

"This place is stunning, I love it."

Phillipe held her hand as he led her up the stairs, past the gorgeous oil paintings on the walls, down a hall into the master bedroom. Closing the door behind them, he waited as Charlotte surveyed the room. There was a huge bed on one side, next to the nearly floor to ceiling windows overlooking the lawn. A dresser took up most of another wall, and a walk in closet and master bath completed the room. She turned expectantly back to Phillipe, saying nothing. Gazing into her eyes, and once again taking her hand, he led her to the master bathroom. She stood in the middle of the room, in front of the large, gilded mirror as Phillipe pulled her close and nuzzled her neck.

"I thought you might find a nice, hot bath soothing." Leaving her momentarily, he walked to the tub and started the water, added some lavender oil to the water, and lit the candles surrounding the tub. Soon, the smell of lavender filled the room as he returned to where Charlotte was standing. Slowly he unbuttoned her blouse, letting it fall to the floor. She was sure he could hear the thudding of her heart, not to mention feel her quivering as he removed her skirt. She stepped out of her shoes and skirt, the marble floor cold to her feet. Phillipe ran his hands up her sides from her waist to her back, unhooking her bra and letting it fall in the pile of clothes on the floor. Gently he fondled her breasts, before bringing his mouth to them, first sucking on one, tongue flicking around the nipple, then the other. Charlotte groaned as she grabbed his head, hands buried in his thick hair. Phillipe slowly sank to his knees, moving his mouth down her stomach, licking and nibbling as he reached her panties, finally pulling them down her legs with his teeth. Slowly he made his way back up her legs, gently pushing them apart with his hands as he kissed his way back up. His mouth settled between her legs, tongue moving all around as he sucked and licked. Charlotte felt her knees going weak and threw her head back as she held tight to his head and soon climaxed. Phillipe stood back up and in one motion, picked her up and carried her to the bath, gently placing her in the water. Without saying a word, he removed his clothes and joined her in the tub.

Phillipe kissed Charlotte deeply, tongues entwining, then he leaned back, pulling her on top of him. Charlotte felt his erection, and grabbed it with one hand and guided him into her, her other hand massaging his testicles. Phillipe's hands back on her breasts, they moved in a rhythm, going faster as she ground into him. Water splashed over the tub as they both came together, waves of ecstasy passed over Charlotte as she shuddered and finally collapsed on top of Phillipe.

"You are so beautiful," Phillipe whispered into her ear as he pulled her close, feeling her heart beating against his chest. Putting his hands on either side of her face, he kissed her again, then wrapped his arms around her and held her, stroking her back as they lay in the warmth of the tub. Charlotte thought she could lie there forever, she couldn't ever remember being so happy.

Soon the water started to cool and they got out of the tub, wrapping themselves in big, fluffy, white towels to dry off. Phillipe again picked Charlotte up and carried her to the bed, laying her down, tossing the towels to the side.

Kiki stared at Charlotte's hand. "I can't believe you're engaged! Look at that ring, it is absolutely gorgeous! Tell me everything!" Charlotte laughed as she recounted her weekend with Phillipe. How he treated her like a princess, the walks around the property, the riding, and of course the sex. Then there was the proposal. They had ridden the horses out through the woods to an open meadow near a stream for a picnic. Phillipe had pulled the ring out of his pocket and gotten down on one knee, professed his love for her and asked her to be his bride. Charlotte had been overwhelmed with love for the first time in her life. She finally felt that everything Kiki had told her was coming true. She could move beyond her past and have a fabulous life with Phillipe. Her reverie was broken when Kiki suddenly exclaimed, "Oh, I forgot, you have a bunch of letters from your father. I think you better read them, they are marked urgent."

Charlotte looked down at the letters Kiki handed her with dread. Suddenly her mood changed and she stared at the letters addressed to her in her father's handwriting and was transported back to the child she had been. Gone was the engaged woman living her own life, ready to stand up to her family. Maybe Kiki was wrong, maybe she couldn't ever get away from her past and the hold it had on her. With trepidation, she opened the most recent letter, postmarked a week ago, and began to read. "Dear Charlotte..."

"Oh no!" she cried, "It's my mother! She is extremely ill, and I need to get home right away!"

23 CHAPTER TWENTY-THREE

Kelly appraised herself in the mirror as people flitted about touching up her hair and gown. "I am actually going through with it", she thought. She was really going to marry Jonathan. Mrs. Kelly Pierce, not a bad name, I guess. Jonathan could be fun, and he certainly was good looking, so maybe it won't be so bad. Silly fool didn't even sign a prenuptial agreement, not that he had any actual money of his own, but he would someday. Charlotte already had been very generous, even paying for this lavish wedding. A small smile crossed her lips, maybe she should marry Charlotte instead. Kelly almost laughed out loud. It doesn't really matter, Charlotte was so easy to figure out, and it was hardly an effort to get money from her. It was pitiful how needy she really was. Charlotte thought she was so in control, but she wasn't. Other people controlled her. Especially when it came to her money. A few kind words and she was all yours. Sad really.

"You should smile, you look absolutely stunning, and so does your soon to be husband. I caught a glimpse of him earlier, he is smoking hot!" Tracy, a friend of Kelly's from college, put the final touches on Kelly's gown. "I think we're done here, so if you're ready, I'll let them know."

Kelly took one last look in the mirror. Smiling, she said, "Yes, I'm

168

ready. Let's go do this."

Jonathan stood nervously at the altar, waiting on Kelly. He was starting to get cold feet, wondering what the hell he was doing. "Why am I marrying her?" he thought, "How in the world did I get sucked into this? How did this happen?" Jonathan had been with many women; always dumping them once he got bored, which generally was pretty fast. How did Kelly manage to get under his skin like that? Yes, she was beautiful, but he'd had many beautiful girlfriends. The sex was great, but he'd had great sex, too. For the life of him, he had no idea how he ended up agreeing to get married. There was something intoxicating about her that he couldn't put his finger on. Was it love? Maybe, but he didn't think so. It was more like an addiction. Maybe it was how smart she was, she knew how to manipulate people almost as well as he did. Actually, since he was standing at the alter waiting on her, maybe she was better. She got him to propose after all. What was the old song his mother would play? Something about, witchcraft, it must be witchcraft. "That must be it, witchcraft, now I finally understand that stupid song."

"I wonder what would happen if I just walked away now," he thought. His mother would probably have a stroke. His siblings would be shocked, or pretend to be. Ellen would spin in circles trying to make it all right. Emily would probably find it funny. Jake and Graham would probably think it funny, too. Jonathan knew that he wasn't well liked, and his wife was liked even less. Her charm worked on Ellen, but fell flat on everyone else, especially Stella. She made it clear without even saying a word she couldn't stand Kelly, although Stella was civil when talking to her. Of course it didn't help that Kelly tried to flirt with Jake and Graham, not that either of them paid much attention. Particularly Graham, he knew a phony when he saw one. And Kelly was a phony. If they only knew the half of it, he laughed to himself.

Before he could act on his plan of abandoning Kelly at the altar, the music started, and he, along with everyone else, turned to watch as Kelly came down the aisle, looking every bit the princess she believed she was. Jonathan heard the gasp as she entered the room and people took in her beauty, and once again, he was under her spell.

"Wasn't that the most beautiful wedding? What a great looking couple," Gina laughed at Graham.

"We all know weddings aren't your thing, Graham."

"It is just so phony. I guess they do make a good couple, they are so much alike. I just wonder why he bothered to marry her. I can guess her reasons, she practically has gold digger in flashing neon lights, but what does he see in her that makes him marry her?"

"That's not the neon lights you see flashing, it's that humongous diamond he gave her," Stella replied.

"You mean Mom gave her," laughed Emily. "There is no way Jonathan could afford that on his own. Does he even have a job these days?"

Jake took a drink and replied, "Maybe he saved up his allowance. What's he get, a grand a week?" They all laughed and then noticed Jonathan and Kelly coming towards them.

"I'm so glad you all were able to make the wedding. It means so much to us to have my family here, right Kelly?" he smiled adoringly at his new bride.

"Of course, I've so exited we are all family now," Kelly replied sweetly. "Oh, they're playing our song, excuse us while we dance." Kelly guided Jonathan to the dance floor.

"Oh my God, I am so going to throw up, that was so sickly sweet," Stella was gagging.

"Stop, you almost made me choke!" laughed Emily. "They are a pair all right. Has anyone talked to Mom yet? Is it safe? You know how she is where her little angel is concerned. Did you see her fawning over them? It makes me want to puke, too."

The others shook their heads. "I haven't," said Jake. "I was going to say something on the way out, which will be soon. I don't know if I can take any more of this crap. Is anyone else ready to go find somewhere where the atmosphere is more normal?"

"Sure, we're about ready to go, too," Said Graham as he and Stella stood up. "We've done our sibling duty, let's hit this pop stand. I think we're done here. We can bid adieu to the old lady on our way out."

24 CHAPTER TWENTY-FOUR

Emily glanced at her watch. "Holy crap! Look what time it is, I can't believe we have been talking so long. I really need to get going if I'm going to help Gail tonight at the bar."

"Yes, you're right, it has gotten late. I can't believe we haven't been thrown out of here," Kiki saw Emily reaching for her wallet, "No, no, no. I have it, I insist." She quickly grabbed the check and placed her credit card on it.

"Thank you, this has been such an emotional, but wonderful day. I have learned so much. I am so glad we met," Emily hugged Kiki. "Please, don't let this be the last time we get together. Remember, you still need to meet the others."

Kiki hugged her back, "I will, I promise. I'll give you some time to take in everything we talked about, and then call me when you are ready. Besides, I have to go tune up my singing skills if I'm going to be in a band again," Kiki laughed and smiled at Emily. The two women gathered their things and walked to their cars. When she reached her car, Kiki turned to Emily. "Are you going to do anything with what I've told you today?"

Emily thought for a moment, and then responded quietly, "I think I'm going to track down Uncle Charles and have a chat with him. He has some explaining to do."

Kiki nodded, and then added, "Please be careful Emily, he may be old, but your uncle is not someone to be taken lightly. There is no telling what he will do if you confront him. I expect he will try to deny it, after all, without Charlotte to back you up, all you have is me. So don't be surprised if you get nowhere, which might be better than if he thinks you have something on him, look what he did to Phillipe after all."

"I'll be careful. I have to think about how I'm going to approach him, what I'll say, but he's not getting away with this any longer," Emily gave Kiki another hug. "Thank you again, you have no idea how much this means to me."

"You are very welcome. We'll be in touch again soon." With that they got into their cars, and with a smile and a wave, they drove off.

Emily called Gail as she drove and excitedly told her about the afternoon with Kiki. "Oh my God Gail, you would not believe it. I can't wait until I get home. I have to tell you everything. And then I have to call Ellen, Graham, and Jake, they are going to flip!" She listened for a bit, then continued. "I should be home soon, and then I'll clean up and change and meet you at the bar. I can fill you in on the rest of it. It was just the most amazing experience. I'm going into a dead zone, I'll talk to you later. I love you, bye!" Hanging up the phone, Emily cranked up the radio, loudly singing for the remainder of her drive.

The next morning Gail was in the kitchen making breakfast when Emily walked in. "You're up early," Gail said as she gave her a quick kiss. "Tea?"

"Yes please, that would be great," Emily sat at the counter watching as Gail poured the tea, added milk and sugar and placed it before Emily. "Thanks," Emily said.

"So, what earth shattering event has you up so early?" smiled Gail.

"I want to talk to Uncle Charles. I couldn't sleep last night thinking about everything Kiki told me. I am still blown away by everything, but mostly I am very angry at Charles. I need to track him down and find out his side, why he did what he did, and if he was the one that killed Phillipe and let mom take the fall. That is just despicable."

"Do you think now is the best time? Should you talk to the others first and see what they say? Maybe you should all get with him, after all, if he did kill Phillipe he could be dangerous," Gail's brow was furrowed with worry. "I don't want to see anything happen to you. Maybe it would be safer if all of you were there."

"I'll be ok, he has to be in his early seventies already. He may not even want to talk to me. I'm not sure yet what I'll say, I don't want to accuse him of anything over the phone, I want to do this in person," Emily picked up a pen and tapped it absentmindedly on the counter. After a few minutes she picked up the phone and started dialing. It took several tries before she located her uncle. Emily was nervous when Charles answered.

"Emily, what a surprise! I'm so sorry about your mother, how are you holding up? Has there been any progress in the investigation?"

"Thank you. They are still following leads. We're all waiting to hear something positive. We really hope they find the killer soon. It's been extremely difficult, as I'm sure you can imagine. Losing your only sister has to have been pretty rough, too."

There was a moment of silence before Charles responded. "Yes, it has been difficult. I loved your mother. It doesn't seem the same without her. I still can't believe it."

Emily cleared her throat, "The reason I called is that I have a lot of questions about Mom and you knew her better than anyone. I've heard some things about her life, but realize I don't really know her. I'd like to meet you and hopefully you can fill in the gaps, if that is okay with you. We can meet wherever it's more convenient for you." Emily held her breath while she waited for Charles to answer.

It seemed to take quite a while before he answered. "Well, I suppose we can do that," Charles answered slowly, "let me check my schedule and we can decide where to meet."

"That would be great, if we could do it as soon as possible, I'd really appreciate it. This has been bugging me for a while and I'd really like to know more about her, who she really was."

"I'll be in touch. It was good to hear from you," Charles said before hanging up the phone.

Gail looked over at Emily, "Well?"

Emily looked puzzled. "I don't know, he doesn't sound happy to hear from me. Maybe I'm just being paranoid, but I don't think he wants to meet with me. I wonder if he really will call back."

"Well, the ball is in his court, you did all you could do. Hopefully he will call. Maybe he just needs some time to think of what he is going to say. After all, it's not like you have been in touch all these years."

"Yeah, it's just going to be hard to wait. It will also be hard if he agrees. Maybe Kiki is right, I should bring someone with me. Now that I've spoken to him, I am a little nervous."

"Maybe Graham can go with you. He seems pretty level headed, not to mention he could protect you if need be. I don't want to see anything happen to you either, remember," Gail looked worriedly at Emily.

"Yeah, I think I'll call him just to see what he has to say."

Stella handed the phone to Graham. "It's Emily."

"Hi Emily, what's up?" Graham asked. He listened as Emily told him about meeting Kiki, and all that Kiki had told her. Graham's fist tightened on the phone receiver as he listened.

"That bastard!" he said. "I can't believe this! Poor mom, no wonder she was so crazy, she didn't stand a chance," He listened again while Emily told of her plan to confront Charles.

"I don't know about this," he said, "We don't know anything about him, and with what you just found out, he could be dangerous."

"That's what Gail said, it's why she said I should call you," Emily responded. "She said you would know what to do, or maybe come with me for protection."

Graham thought for a moment before responding. "Let me think about this. Right now, if I went up there I'm not sure I wouldn't beat the shit out of him for what he did, I'm so pissed. Did you have any idea when you would want to go see him?"

"I called and he said he would check his schedule and get back to me. I'd like to get up there sometime this week, if possible."

"Ok, let's give him a couple of days to see if he sets something up. If he doesn't, we'll just go up there. I don't know if you should tell him I'm coming with you, just in case that scares him off. I'd like to hear what his excuse is for what he did, that son of a bitch."

"Thanks Graham, I feel better knowing you'll be there. Do you think we should tell that detective about this? If it's true he killed her husband, shouldn't he be charged?"

"I don't think anything can be done about it now, it didn't even happen here in te the States. As much as I'd like to see him go down for what he did, unfortunately, I don't think there is anything he can do, so for now at least, I don't think we need to tell him. If something comes up after we talk to Charles, then we can always call Parker and let him know and if there is anything he could be charged with, they can do it."

"Ok, thanks again. I'll let you know in a couple of days whether or not I hear from Charles." Emily and Graham talked for a bit longer before hanging up. Stella looked quizzically at

Graham.

"Dare I ask?" she inquired.

Graham scowled as he told her what Emily said.

"Oh my God!" Stella was stunned. "What a dirt bag! How are you going to go see him and not want to beat the crap out of him?"

"I don't know."

Charles mind raced as he hung up the phone. The call from Emily had definitely unnerved him. Why after all these years is she trying to make contact? Was it really just to learn more about her mother, or did she already know too much? He had to think before he called her back, something in her tone suggested she wasn't going to take no for an answer. The last thing he needed was to have all the mess stirred up again. He was going to have to come up with something to tell Emily, something that would satisfy her so she would go away. What if she wanted to know about Phillipe? He was pretty sure anything they heard implicated Charlotte. That was so long ago, he could barely remember it. One thing was for certain, there was no way he was going to tell them the truth.

25 CHAPTER TWENTY-FIVE

"Forged?" Parker was taking notes, scribbling furiously. "How do you know it's been forged? Do you know who did it?" he listened to the lawyer on the other end of the phone. "So, do you have the original copy?" he listened again before responding. "Sure, I know where your office is, I am on my way," Parker hung up the phone. "Hey Kenny," he called out.

"What's up?"

"Charlotte's lawyer just called. It seems the will giving everything to her youngest son is a forgery. He has the real one in his office. Come on, this should be good. If it turns out Jonathan forged the will to give himself everything, it makes for a pretty good motive for murder. Wouldn't you agree?" Parker already had his keys in his hand and was heading out the door.

Kenny jumped up, following him, "It sure does, I'm right behind you."

Parker and Kenny walked into the law office of Martin and Martin and stopped at the front desk. A neatly dressed young woman with short dark hair and glasses looked up as they approached.

"Can I help you?" She inquired.

"Detectives Williams and Mann to see Bradley Martin," Parker responded.

"Of course, Detective, right this way." The woman got up and escorted them to an office with a frosted glass window on the door. Bradley Martin, Esquire was inscribed on the window. The woman knocked softly and opened the door. "Detectives Williams and Mann to see you sir," she announced as she opened the door.

"Thank you," Parker told her as she stood aside allowing them to enter. She smiled before returning to her desk.

"Come in gentlemen," Bradley Martin rose from behind his desk. He appeared to be in his middle thirties, average height, receding hairline with hair cut very short, dark brown eyes and an easy smile. "Call me Brad," he said as he shook hands with Parker and Kenny. After introductions, they sat in comfortable, plush chairs in front of the huge, mahogany desk. "Can I get you coffee or anything?"

"No thank you," Parker said. "You said on the phone you had been Mrs. Pierce's lawyer for most of her life. Unless you found the fountain of youth, you don't seem old enough to have done that. "

Brad laughed easily. "My father started the business, he was actually her lawyer for many years. Once I came on board, I took over for him and have handled her business ever since," Brad was serious again. "I can't believe she's dead. How horrible. Do you know who killed her, yet?"

Parker shook his head. "We're still following up all the leads. What can you tell me about the will? How did you find out it was forged?"

"Well, as you may or may not know, her son Jake is contesting the will. When I first heard that, I didn't understand why. The will I have leaves everything to her first four kids equally. I thought maybe I misunderstood and Jonathan was the one contesting, because he wasn't in it. I called Graham, since he is the executor of her estate, and he told me he saw the copy leaving everything to Jonathan. I told him I wasn't aware of that copy, so I went to see what had been filed with the county, and sure enough, there it was," Brad handed Parker and Kenny the will.

"So you're saying your office didn't write this one up? Is it possible she went elsewhere and had it done?"

"No way. As I said, we had been handling her affairs for most of her life. There is no way she would go to someone else. Charlotte could be a royal pain in the ass, but she was loyal almost to a fault. Once she established a relationship, as long as you didn't question her too much, or try to tell her what to do, she was fine. We knew how to handle her so she didn't blow through all her money. Charlotte is also the reason I moved here from New York. My father still has the business up there; when Charlotte moved here, we decided it would be easier to handle her down here. I also represent everyone but Jonathan, so it made sense to relocate," Brad looked at the will, "It's pretty obvious this one is forged, even the notary appears forged. It won't take long to verify all that, that's pretty easy, actually."

Parker thought for a moment, studying the will. "Everything

I heard about her was she favored her youngest son, giving him and his wife tons of money over the years. Why did she write him out of the will?"

"She came in here one day recently, all in a lather. Apparently she found out some things about Kelly that set her off, I don't know what it was. All I know is she was furious. She didn't tell me what had happened, but she was adamant that they be taken out of the will. She did admit they had played her for a fool and she was not happy about that in the least. She said it finally hit her how Jonathan and Kelly didn't really give a damn about her, that they had gotten enough all these years, and she was going to give everything to her other kids to try and make up for how she treated them. She wanted them cut off completely, she even stopped the monthly checks she had been sending them."

"How did they handle getting cut off, and did they know about the will?" Parker asked.

"Jonathan called me when he didn't receive a check and he was quite pissed off. He wanted to know what the deal was, and accused me of being behind it. I told him he needed to take it up with his mother. I was just doing what she requested. He asked about the will, and I told him that was confidential information and he would need to talk to her about that, too. He was being a real prick about it, excuse my language. "

"What I don't understand is, let's say Jonathan, or even Kelly, forged a copy of the will. He knew you handled her affairs. Wouldn't you question another will? You have the legitimate copy, how did they think they would get away with it?"

"Good question, but if it wasn't for me hearing about Jake

contesting it, it may have slipped by. Even Graham thought it was a real one and since she doted on Jonathan, Graham just accepted it as real. Greed will make people do all sorts of things, as I'm sure you know."

Parker nodded, "Yes, you're right. We see how nasty people can be when money is involved. Well, this does change things, if nothing else, sounds like some fraud charges will be filed when we figure out who did this. Can we keep this copy?"

"Sure, and if you need anything else, let me know. Like I said, I've known Charlotte pretty much my whole life. I hope you get whoever is responsible, she had a rough life despite her wealth, and she didn't deserve getting killed."

"Thanks Brad, you've been a big help. I'll be in touch," Parker and Kenny shook hands with Brad and started towards the door when Parker stopped and turned back to Brad.

"Oh, one other question. You said you handled all the family, except Jonathan. Can I ask why?"

"Sure, like I said, he's a prick. Even us lawyers have standards on occasion," Brad laughed. "Let me tell you, if I had to pick a suspect, Jonathan and Kelly would be top of the list. There is something not quite right with those two. Hey look, some of the others may have issues with money, but their mother would always take care of it if things got bad. They aren't bad people. I don't see them trying to off their mother for the money. Now they might get so pissed off at her over something stupid and who knows, but my money is still on the other two. As far as I'm concerned, they have no compassion or concern for anyone but themselves."

Graham nodded and said, "Well, thanks again for your help. We'll be in touch if we have any further questions."

"You're welcome," Brad replied, then slapped his forehead with his hand, "Oh wait, there is something else. I don't know if you are already aware, but Jonathan has a child with another woman that lives in Roanoke. I don't know if anyone else knows about it. I know Kelly doesn't. Since he's not my client, I'm not giving up any privileged information. I can't tell you where I heard it though, and I'm pretty sure Charlotte wasn't even aware of it. I don't know if he ever visits the kid, but it might be something to check out." Brad wrote on a piece of paper and handed it to Parker. "Like I said, I can't tell you how I found out, that would be confidential information, but this is the name and address of the child's mother."

Parker read what was written on the paper, and said, "Thanks again Brad, are you sure you don't want to switch careers and become a cop?"

Brad laughed, "Nah, I like what I do, even if it is pretty boring most days. But I must admit, this has added some excitement to the day, so you never know."

"Well, just let us know if you ever change your mind, I think you have a knack for police work," Parker and Kenny smiled and left the office.

They left the building and as they got into the car, Kenny said, "It looks like we have our prime suspects. Funny, I don't remember Jonathan mentioning another child, do you? Especially not one living less than an hour away from our murder scene. I think it's time for another chat with him, don't you? "

"Yeah, we'll have to interview him again, but first I think we swing by and have a chat with the mother of his child. See if he's been here. Let's also get his cell phone records and see if we can place him in the area during the time of the murder. "

"I'm on it," Kenny replied as he picked up his phone.

* * *

Sally peeked out the window before opening the door, noticing the unmarked car in the driveway. *What the crap are the cops doing here,* she wondered. *This better not be something Jonathan has done after their last blow up.* She opened the door as Kenny was getting ready to knock again.

"Can I help you?" she asked.

"Are you Sally?" inquired Parker.

"Yes. What is this about?"

Parker introduced himself and Kenny. "We are investigating a murder and would like to ask you a few questions. May we come in?"

"A murder? I don't know anything about a murder!" Sally looked at the detectives.

"This won't take long. Please, may we come in?" Parker persisted. Sally glanced again at both men, and then opened the door to allow them in.

"I'm sure you're mistaken," she continued as she showed them to the living room. "Have a seat. Excuse the mess, I wasn't expecting company and haven't had time to straighten up."

Parker and Kenny glanced around the small room, littered with toys. "How many kids do you have?" asked Kenny.

"Just one, if you can believe it. But it seems like more at times. Chloe! Come pick up your toys!" Sally yelled. "Kids, I swear." Sally moved some magazines off a chair and sat down, watching nervously as Parker and Kenny sat on the couch, Kenny immediately half rising as he removed a toy from the cushion before sitting again.

Parker began, "As I mentioned, we are investigating a murder. Do you know Jonathan Pierce?"

Sally's hand flew up to her mouth, "Oh my God, is he dead?"

"No", replied Kenny.

"Oh, that's too bad." Sally settled back down. "He's a drunken, stupid mistake I made. The only good thing from my short time with Jonathan is my daughter, Chloe," Sally looked sullen. "So, who was murdered?"

Kenny and Parker exchanged a glance. "His mother, Charlotte," Kenny replied. "Did you know her?"

"No, I never met any of his family. Like I said, it was not much more than a one night stand, defiantly not a big romance."

Parker let Kenny continue the questioning, "When was the last time you saw or heard from Jonathan?"

"It was a couple of weeks ago. I had been calling him to get him to send the child support. The asshole has all this money and he cheaps out when it comes to his own kid. I told him if he didn't send a check, I was going to call Kelly and his mother and introduce myself, and let them know about Chloe. He flew into a rage, started screaming at me, called me every name in the book, threatened me, you name it."

"He threatened you?" Parker interrupted.

"Yes, he always did when he got mad enough. He was either going to, break every bone in my body, or kill me and hide my body so no one would ever find me."

"Did you take him seriously? Ever report him to the police?" Kenny asked.

"Yes, and no. The police aren't going to do anything, he lives out of state. I have a gun, and know how to use it. He tries anything and he's going to be so full of holes, he drinks a glass of water and it'll be pouring out all the holes."

Parker and Kenny looked at each other, not sure what to make of Sally. "Well, you said Jonathan showed up, I'm assuming he's not leaking water?" Kenny asked.

Sally smiled, "You're funny. No, I was prepared but he had calmed down so I saved my ammunition. It's hard to come by these days, you know. Anyway, he was civil. He paid what he owed and took off. Though he did remind me I was not to let Kelly or his family know about the kid. Honestly, I don't care if they know or not, as long as he keeps up with the child support. It's such a pain chasing him down for it."

"Do you know what date he came down and how long he stayed? And where he stayed?"

"I'm not sure the exact date. I can get that for you. I believe he came down two weeks ago on a Friday night. He was here Sunday to give me the check, he didn't even want to see Chloe, just gave me the check and left."

"So you didn't see him Friday or Saturday, any idea where he was?" Kenny asked.

"No, not a clue. He was probably sucking up to his mother to get the money. The check was from his mother, I don't know what story he gave her to make it out to me. I'm sure he did it that way so Kelly wouldn't see it and question anything."

Kenny was having a hard time containing his excitement. "Do you have a copy of the check?"

"Actually, I do. I made one for tax purposes. I can make you a copy if you need one."

"That would be great," Kenny said.

Sally stood up, "hang on just a sec and I'll be right back."

Parker and Kenny smiled at each other as she left the room. "This could be our first big break. The check will have a date on it, and we can prove he was in the area. Not to mention motive."

Sally returned and handed them the copy. "Here you go. How does all this help with your investigation? Do you think Jonathan killed his mother?"

"We're just following all the leads right now. Do you think he's capable of murder?" Kenny asked.

"I don't know. He has a temper, that's a fact. But I'm not sure if he could actually kill anyone. And why would he kill his mother? He is broke without her support. Now Kelly, she's another story. I never met her, but from what Jonathan tells me, you don't cross her. If she's married to him, she has to be one cold hearted bitch if he's afraid of her."

Kenny paused in his note taking, "Is he afraid of her? Did he ever say that?"

"Not in so many words, but he goes to great lengths to keep me a secret. We hooked up while they were separated. You would think he would have balls enough to tell her, hey , it was after she left him, but no, he insists on keeping it a secret. He did say she has quite the temper, too."

Parker and Kenny put their notepads away, and Kenny handed Sally his card. "Here is my number, call me if you think of anything else that might be helpful. Thank you for your time."

Sally smiled seductively at Kenny, "You bet."

They left the house with Sally watching them from the door. They got in the car and Kenny waved to Sally as they pulled away.

"Nice job Romeo," Parker laughed as Kenny blushed.

"Hey, I can't help if my animal magnetism shines through. Don't be jealous. Besides, you have Kate, remember?"

Parker smiled, "Like I could ever forget. Ok, let's go grab something to eat, and see where we stand. We'll have to get bank records from Charlotte and Jonathan, see how many other checks there are. Once we get the phone records, and find out where he stayed when he was here, we can start to piece this thing together.

I'm feeling good about this. I love it when a case comes together."
They high fived each other and drove down the road, smiling.

Back at the station, Parker and Kenny returned to their desks
and began making calls, tracking down the cell phone and bank
records, as well as hotels in search of where Jonathan stayed.
Kenny also worked to track down plane reservations and car
rentals. It was late in the afternoon when Kenny jumped up.

"Got it!" he whooped. "He flew into Roanoke on Friday,
stayed at the Hotel Roanoke, of course, and flew out on Sunday
night. I have everyone faxing me the records, we should have it
all shortly."

"Good work," Parker said. "Once you get those records, I say
we call it a night. We can start putting this all together in the
morning, go from there. I think we hop a flight and do a face to
face interview with Jonathan, unless we can get him to come here.
Maybe we can use the will as an excuse to get him here. It would
be easier to arrest him if he's on our turf. "

"Yeah, maybe we can get Brad to call and tell him there is a
problem with the will and he needs to be here in person. I'll bet
that gets his butt down here."

"Good idea, I'll call Brad in the morning and set it up. In the
meantime, I'm going to head on out, don't stay too long, we need
to be fresh for tomorrow, I think it's going to be an intense day."

"Okay, have a good night and I'll see you bright and early
tomorrow," Kenny said as he watched Parker leave, then walked
over to the fax machine whistling, which started humming as

papers began to spew out.

* * *

The next morning Parker was already at his desk and on the phone when Kenny came in.

"Thanks Brad, you did great. We'll be by in a couple of hours," Parker hung up the phone and looked over at Kenny. "Brad called Jonathan, and as expected, hearing there was an issue with the will got his attention. Both he and Kelly are on the way. Their flight lands at noon, so we have some time to arrange things. We'll head over to Brad's office and wait for them. We can discuss how to play this, I have a feeling Kelly may be the one to watch out for. She seems more cunning than Jonathan. I think he's more volatile, but once they find out about the will, and maybe even Sally and Chloe, there is no telling what will happen. I think we need to be prepared for anything."

Kenny nodded. "So, good cop, bad cop?"

Parker thought a minute. "I think so, but, I think it's also better the less we say. Keep in mind these are not stupid people we are dealing with, they are both very calculating. Let's try to keep it brief and see if they hang themselves."

"You're the boss," Kenny replied. "I'll follow your lead. Of course, if Kelly should fall under my spell, I can't control that."

Parker rolled his eyes. "I guess we'll just have to deal with it if it happens. Now, let's get a move on, I want to go over with Brad what might happen before they show up."

"Oh, I meant to tell you. You don't have to worry about Karen anymore."

"Oh? Why not?" asked Parker.

"I heard she and another medic were caught doing the nasty in the back of one of the ambulances while they were on duty. They were both fired and Karen is moving back to North Carolina to live with her mother. It appears you and Kate are now free to pursue you relationship in peace," Kenny smiled over at Parker.

"Man, you just made my day," laughed Parker. "Now let's go bag a killer."

Kelly drummed her fingers on the counter while Jonathan dealt with the car rental agent. Finally, the paperwork done, Jonathan picked up the key and they headed to the terminal doors. They didn't speak until after the car was out of the airport and on the highway, heading to Brad's office.

"You said there wouldn't be a problem," Kelly glared at Jonathan." You swore this would be a piece of cake. No one will know, you said. So what could be the problem?" Kelly stared daggers at Jonathan.

"Would you shut up already? We don't know what the issue is. As long as you don't blow it I am sure this won't be a big deal. I can handle this. I said you didn't need to be here." Jonathan scowled at Kelly, and then looked straight ahead again. They didn't speak again until they pulled up and parked outside Brad's office.

"Let me handle this. I don't want you saying anything, is that clear?" Jonathan glowered at Kelly.

"Whatever," Kelly gave herself a final check in the mirror before opening the car door. "You better not screw this up. We have too much at stake for you to blow it."

"I told you, I will handle it. Now just put your good girl face on and let's get this over with," Jonathan slammed his door and moving to the front of the car he took Kelly's arm and together they walked into the office.

"We're here to see Mr. Martin," Jonathan announced to the woman behind the desk.

"Just a moment, please. I'll let him know you're here," she replied as she picked up the phone. "Mr. and Mrs. Pierce to see you," she said into the receiver. After a moment she replied, "Yes sir, I'll send them in." Getting up from her desk she escorted Jonathan and Kelly to Brad's office. "Right this way please," she said as she opened the door, allowing them to enter before quietly closing the door behind them.

Jonathan and Brad shook hands and Brad pointed to the chairs in front of his desk. "Please, have a seat. Hopefully this won't take long. I'm sure it's just a mistake."

"What is the problem?" Jonathan asked.

"Well, it seems that the will that you filed isn't the same one that I have here. As you know, I'm your mother's attorney and the will that she had done just a few months ago is not the same one that you filed. I'm sure you weren't aware she had a new will, and thought you had the correct one." Brad tapped the paper on his desk.

"The one we filed is the correct one. My mother gave it to me herself. She was afraid if the others saw it, since I was inheriting everything, they would go ballistic and try to contest it. Which of course is what happened anyway," Jonathan sighed and slowly shook his head. "I guess I understand how they feel, but Mother always told me how they were only after her money, and how I was the only one that cared for her. She wanted to be sure I was taken care of after my father abandoned me as a baby."

Brad tried not to roll his eyes. "That's funny, because she told me exactly the opposite when she was in here. She was quite specific about who was to inherit, and in fact, she told me in no uncertain terms, you were not to inherit a dime as you have already gotten more than enough all these years. Here is a copy," he said as he handed it to Jonathan.

"WHAT?" Kelly exploded out of her seat. "You are lying! There is no way she would do that! Those bastards are behind this, aren't they?"

"Kelly sit down and shut up!" Jonathan yelled. "I told you to let me handle this! Obviously this is a fake," turning back to Brad he continued, "I don't know what kind of game you are trying to pull here, but this is not correct. I've already filed the real will, this is just bullshit. "

Brad stared at Jonathan and Kelly, "You can think what you want, but I can prove the one you filed is a fake. And it doesn't matter what you think. I know this is the real one, and that is the one that will be honored. Sorry, but you aren't inheriting a damn thing."

This time Jonathan got to his feet, and towered over Brad, who remained seated. "Listen you son of a bitch. If you are insinuating that I faked a will and filed it, I'll sue your ass for libel. You won't be able to practice law anywhere when I get done with you."

"Actually, it will be tough to do that from jail. Filing a forged will is quite illegal," Brad seemed nonplussed. "Now if you will sit your ass down maybe we can continue."

"There is nothing to continue. I'm done," Jonathan turned to leave.

"Is that why you killed your mother, for the money?" Brad asked.

Jonathan spun around and in one swift move grabbed Brad by the throat and lifting him out of the chair, pinned him against the wall. "What did you just say?" he growled at him.

"Jonathan!" Kelly yelled, "Stop it!"

Just then the door opened and Parker and Kenny entered, guns drawn. "Let him go, now!" yelled Parker. "Hands behind your back," Parker commanded as Jonathan released Brad and turned toward Parker. "I said, hands behind your back!" Parker repeated as Jonathan slowly turned around.

"What do you think you're doing?" cried Kelly. "Leave him alone, you can't arrest him!"

"He assaulted Mr. Martin," Parker replied as he put the handcuffs on Jonathan. "That's just for starters. There is also the matter of filing a forged will, which in this case is also grand larceny. Let's go," he said as he and Kenny holstered their guns and began to escort Jonathan out of the office. "Are you ok Brad?"

Brad nodded. "Just a little shook up and sore. I don't think any major damage was done."

"Let us know if you need to have us call an ambulance, or if you want to see a doctor," Kenny responded.

"Oh no, I think I'm ok, but thanks," Brad replied, holding his throat.

"You bastards, I'll have your badges, too!" Jonathan sputtered with rage. "My attorney will be outraged at this, it's false arrest!"

"You have the right to remain silent," Parker began as he recited the Miranda rights to Jonathan. "Do you understand your rights as I have read them to you?"

"Fuck you," Jonathan replied as they led him out of the office and placed him in the back of the patrol car. "Kelly, get our attorney on the phone. This is bullshit."

"Don't worry, you said. I'll handle this, you said. Great job handling it," Kelly glared at Jonathan.

"Shut up and call the lawyer." Jonathan glared back.

Parker and Kenny got in the car and with Jonathan muttering curses at them, drove off towards the jail.

Later, after Jonathan had been booked and taken to a cell to wait on his attorney, Parker and Kenny sat in Parker's office.

"Well, that didn't go exactly as planned. However, did you

see how fast he was on Brad? He certainly has a quick temper, and gets violent. Suppose Charlotte told him to meet her on the trail, thinking since it was a public place she would be safe, and then told him about the new will?" Kenny looked over at Parker.

"It's definitely possible. Poor Brad, that could have gotten really ugly. I'm glad we were there, I'd hate to think what would happen if we weren't. I don't think Kelly would have been much help."

"She is a piece of work. Did you see her eyeing me as we left?" Kenny opened a bottle of water. "I think now that her hubby has been disinherited, she might be on the make for her next one."

Parker rolled his eyes and groaned. "Don't get your hopes up, I know how much you make and believe me, you can't afford her. Our salaries combined wouldn't get a lunch date with that one."

Kenny feigned disappointment. "Damn. Oh well, I guess it's back to work. It's too bad Jonathan lawyered up. I'd really like to get his story. It might be interesting if we could get Kelly to come down for a chat. Maybe now that she realizes they are not getting all that dough, she might be willing to turn him in. Unless of course she had some involvement."

"I already tried, she's not talking, either," Parker absently tapped on his desk with a pen. "We'll just have to keep digging. Jonathan will probably be out tomorrow morning, I'm sure he'll be able to post bond. Though of course Kelly might decide to let him chill for a bit. Things didn't sound so peachy between them."

"I told you, she wants someone with authority, a man that can handle a situation like that calmly," Kenny preened.

Parker laughed, "Whatever dreamboat, get back to work."

"Hey Kenny, package for you on your desk," the receptionist called out as Kenny headed to his office. He saw that Parker had once again beaten him in this morning.

"Thanks," he said, picking up the large manila envelope. Pulling out the contents, Kenny realized it was Charlotte's phone records. Sitting down he excitedly went through them. As expected, he soon found Jonathan's number showing up multiple times. "Probably asking for money, and setting up her coming to the trail to get the child support check," he mused. Then after Jonathan's number, another number stood out. There was an outgoing call the day Charlotte had disappeared. That didn't make sense. If she was already meeting Jonathan, why is she still home making calls? Something was niggling at him. Pulling her file out, he searched to see if there was a match for the number. After a few minutes, he found the match.

"Hey Parker," he called out. "You need to see this, we may have a problem."

* * *

Graham pulled into Emily's driveway and parked the car. He was almost to the door when Emily opened it.

"Come on in," she said, stepping to the side to allow him to enter. "I am so nervous about this, how about you?"

"I'm ok right now. We'll see what happens when I see him face to face. I can't guarantee I won't do something I'll regret if he starts talking," Emily saw Graham was not in the best of moods.

"Do I need to have Parker come along to prevent you from killing him?" she asked only half- jokingly.

"I thought about that, but I think it will be ok. Are you ready? I want to get this over with."

"Yeah," she said grabbing her purse, "let's go. You're driving. I don't think I can focus right now."

Charles paced the room. Even at seventy one, he was still very fit, working out every day and watching what he ate. Charles was determined not to be like others in his age group, who decided to give in to age, always complaining about all the aches and pains and illness they suffered from. If they just watched their diet and worked out, they wouldn't need all those medications, he thought. He stopped to admire himself in the mirror. He was proud that he wore the same size as when he was in his thirties, not to mention he could lift the same amount of weight and bench-press the same amount as when he was younger. The only concession he made to his age was running. He had to admit he wasn't quite as fast as he used to be, but at least he could still run.

People were always surprised when they found out how old he was as he could easily pass for much younger.

His thoughts returned to Emily's upcoming visit. Stay calm, just stick to the story and everything will be fine. Except of course that everything wasn't fine. Charlotte was dead. The reality hit him like a ton of bricks and he fought back tears as the pain and emptiness hit him. Even though they had been estranged for many years, he still loved her and knowing she was gone was tough for him to bear .If only she had listened to him, she might still be alive.

* * *

Parker reviewed the phone records with Kenny, his brow furrowed as he concentrated. Finally he walked to the wall, which was covered in long sheets of blank white poster paper. Picking up a black marker, he started to write on the paper.

"Ok, let's start over. Here are all the suspects," he said as he first wrote each family member's name at the top, then added Kevin the ax murderer. "Let's review everyone's alibi and the other evidence and see who we can cross off. First we have Jake and Gina. What do we know about them?"

"Live in New York, Jake has a temper, they are having financial difficulties."

"Alibi?"

"They are both up there, he just lost his job so he was home working on resumes, she was helping. We have no evidence that he was in this area, no plane tickets, car rentals, or hotels." Parker finished writing what Kenny reported under their names.

"Ok next we have Graham and Stella."

"Both live nearby, admit strained relationship with Charlotte. Both mountain bikers and are familiar with the trails. Graham seems quiet, but by all accounts he can have a temper, too. He was working with his partner. She claims she was at the farm or running errands."

"Ellen and Daniel. Tell me about them."

"He has issues with alcohol and gambling. Bad business decisions along with the gambling debts have put them in a financial bind. Had been separated, recently reconciled. No real alibi for either. He claims he was working at home, she backs him up."

Parker finished writing.

"Emily and Gail".

"Own a bar together, seems to be doing well. Not as much financial trouble as the others, though they have a fair amount of debt from starting the bar. Both were working, I was only able to verify Gail was there all night. Emily was there early, but no one could vouch for her after that. They are in a relationship that Charlotte wasn't aware of, and would have had issues with. I'm not sure that is reason to kill, but these days you never know. Could have been an act of passion."

"Ok, let's stick to facts, not what we think happened yet. Our favorites, Jonathan and Kelly."

"Do you have enough room to write about them?" Kenny smiled. "Jonathan. Spoiled by his mother his whole life. Has a temper. Had been separated from Kelly for a bit and had a kid with someone else. Wife doesn't know about the kid. He is milking mom to pay the child support. We have phone, car rental and hotel records that he was in the area at the time of the murder. We also have a witness to prove he was here. Not to mention we have a check Charlotte wrote that day for the child support, so we know he had contact with her. He forges a will giving himself fifteen million dollars and files it. They try to alibi each other, but as we know, his is bogus. So far nothing showing up to prove she was here."

"Kevin Whitman."

"I verified he is still in prison, no screw ups with him being released by mistake or anything. I think he is ok to cross off the list."

"Agree. Which brings us to Charles."

"Half- brother who we thought lived in Connecticut, but is really in Maryland. It took me a while to track him down for his interview. Only four hours away. Estranged from his sister, no one knows why. Claims he was home, no one to verify so we are just taking the word of a seventy year old man. Says he hasn't seen or talked to Charlotte in years, yet the day she is likely murdered, his phone number shows up. He does have children from a previous marriage, though from what I can tell, they don't live with him, so it doesn't appear anyone else would be calling."

Parker finished writing and turned to Kenny.

"Ok, Jake and Gina. What's your feeling, keep them on the

board or eliminate as suspect?"

"I say we can cross them off. He might be a loose cannon, but we have zero evidence that he was in the area so no opportunity."

"Done. Graham and Stella. They have opportunity. What's your take?"

"I don't see it. There is no real motive. Graham was the only one to think the money was going to Jonathan, so there is no financial gain. Stella may not have gotten along with Charlotte, but I just don't see her as a killer. Both are physically capable, but where is the motive? I say eliminate."

"Yeah, I agree. Ellen and Daniel?"

"Their alibis aren't that great, they have motive, but honestly, I think he's too lazy. Plus I think if he called Charlotte and asked to meet somewhere, she would be suspicious. I don't feel Ellen is capable, either and we really don't have any evidence on either."

Parker crossed out their names. "Emily and Gail."

"Gail is pretty solid on the alibi. Emily most likely is, too, though there seems to be a window of opportunity. I don't see the motive. Yeah, there is debt, but the business is doing well, so they should be able to handle that. And I just don't see the relationship being a motive. I say cross them off."

"Agreed. So, that brings us back to Jonathan and Kelly, and now Charles."

"As much as I don't like Kelly, and think she is capable, I think she is more of a manipulator. She is the type that would have someone else do her killing. We have nothing to prove she was here, either. Jonathan had the motive, and the opportunity, especially if Charlotte threatened him with telling Kelly about the kid. I don't think that would go over well. I still like him."

"Ok, cross off Kelly, but keep Jonathan. That brings us to Charles. And that isn't including anyone else we don't even know about yet. I think we need to pay Charles a visit. I'd like to know why he's suddenly talking to his sister after all these years, especially on the day she was murdered."

"I agree. Are we going now?"

"No time like the present. Let's hope this doesn't take us in a whole different direction. The way this case is going, who knows," Parker said as he gathered up his car keys and headed out the door.

Graham and Emily pulled up to the estate and parked in front of the huge house. Graham shut off the car and they looked at each other.

"You ready?" Emily asked him.

"About as ready as I'll ever be. Come on," Getting out of the car, they walked up the front walkway, ascended the wide, cement steps to the spacious covered entryway and rang the bell. They heard the chimes deep within the house, and about a minute later, the door opened and Charles stood before them. No one spoke as he looked first at Graham, and then Emily.

"The staff has the day off. Come in." Graham and Emily entered, and waited as Charles closed the door behind them. "We can talk in here," he said as he led them to the library. "Can I get you anything? Coffee, tea, something stronger?"

"No thank you," both politely declined as they took their seats in front of a massive, mahogany desk. Sitting behind the desk, Charles looked at both for a moment before speaking.

"I'm so sorry about your mother. It is such a tragedy. Have the police found the killer yet?"

"Thank you," Graham replied. "Jonathan has been arrested for assault on her lawyer, and for filing a forged will. I don't know if he's been charged yet for her murder."

"Jonathan. Why doesn't that surprise me? She should never have kept that child, but as usual, your mother didn't listen to what anyone told her. If she had, she might still be alive."

Emily glanced over at Graham before speaking, "Why do you say that?"

Charles focused on Emily, "You look so much like your mother, has anyone ever told you? You don't have her hair of course. She had that beautiful, long, blond hair. It made her look angelic, though of course we know how she really was. To answer your question, my dear, your mother made some very poor choices in her life. When things didn't work out as expected, she blamed others, even though it was her own doing. She would never accept blame. She liked to play the victim. For years she got away with it. Poor Charlotte, is what everyone always said, such a tragic life, they would say. And yet, it was all her own doing," Charles slowly shook his head. "Father and I would try to help her, try to keep her from doing wrong, but it didn't do any good. She was a constant embarrassment to the family, and I do hold her responsible for our father's death," Charles paused before continuing.

"I'm sure you came here to hear stories of what a wonderful person she was, but I'm sorry. I can't give that to you. When she was a child, she was a lovely creature. Unfortunately as she got older, and maybe it was the times we lived in, she tried to be something she could never be. Charlotte was born to be an heiress, nothing more. She would never be independent. She was too spoiled and lazy. Look how she raised you kids. Our father was beside himself, as was yours. Poor Victor, he didn't stand a chance, though he tried his hardest."

Emily cleared her throat, "I ran into Kiki the other day. She was at mom's grave site."

Charles snorted, "Ah yes, Kiki. I wondered what happened to her. Let me guess, she gave you some sob story about your mother and that's why you are here," Emily and Graham exchanged a glance. "I thought so," Charles noted. "Let me tell you about Kiki .She is probably the reason your mother turned out like she did. Kiki was a very bad influence on your mother. It was Kiki that turned your mother away from her family. It was Kiki that got your mother smoking dope and whoring around Europe with her band. So, tell me, what lies has Kiki fed you?" Charles looked expectantly at his guests.

"Uh, well," Emily started.

"Let's start with the rape," Graham glared, steely eyes boring into Charles.

Charles sighed, "I should have guessed. Yes, the so called rape.
You won't like what I have to say, but please hear me out.
Charlotte was pretty much raised by herself. I was older, and was
away at school. We only saw each other during summer and
holidays. Her mother didn't have much to do with her, nor did
our father. It just wasn't the way it was done back then, especially
in wealthy families. Charlotte craved attention from the time she
was born. She was such a beautiful, endearing child, but then she
started to grow up. Even though I was away at school, I'd hear the
rumors of her and how she acted around men. Several of father's
friends were uncomfortable around her. She would sit in their
laps and hug them when they visited. When she was a child, that
was acceptable, but when she was still doing it as she got to be
around ten, it was embarrassing. Father told her mother to speak
to her about it, and change her behavior. I think it worked for the
friends of my father, but then she started on the young men on the
staff," Charles paused, and looked contrite. "I'm not proud of
myself for what happened. You have to remember I was only
sixteen at the time. I returned home that summer and Charlotte
was excited to see me, as I was her. Even though we didn't see
each other often, we were best friends and I adored her. Anyway,
I get home and she is dressed in shorts and a shirt, flaunting her
body. We decide to go to the beach and have a picnic. I should
have known better, but like I said, I was young and stupid. I
offered her wine, which we drank too much of. She began
throwing herself at me, rubbing all over me, and I'm ashamed to
say, I took advantage. There was no rape, it was consensual. Of
course after she realized the trouble she would be in, not only for
what she did, but also being drunk, she tried to change her story.
I told her no one would believe her, look at the way she acted all
the time. She eventually realized I was right, and I never heard

anything about it until she met Kiki. I'm sure it was her way to remove the shame and guilt of her behavior, but it wasn't true."

Graham did a slow burn, "And you expect us to believe that crap?" Emily nodded.

"I don't care if you believe it or not. I'm sure if you start to think about all your mother's boyfriends and realize how much she loved sex, you'd see the truth," snapped Charles. "I've had to live with this my whole life, under a cloud of suspicion, all because of her."

"What about her husband? What happened to him?" Emily asked.

Charles sighed. "Kiki again, I bet. She probably has me murdering him for who knows what reason. That woman is intolerable, always was. She disliked me from the beginning, probably because I wouldn't chase after her. She wasn't used to that, she was used to men falling all over her, at least until she started hanging out with Charlotte. After that, the only one all the men wanted was Charlotte. Poor Kiki."

"Well?" pressed Emily. "What happened to Phillipe?"

"Let me think, that was so long ago."

The waves lapped gently against the side of the Tendresse as it sat tied to the dock .It was a beautiful day, the air was clear, a light breeze was blowing, the water crystal blue. Charlotte hung over the rail taking in the smell of the sea, and letting the wind blow softly through her hair. She heard the sound of the guests approaching, laughing and talking excitedly. She listened to the sound of the different accents when she was startled by a familiar voice behind her.

"Good morning Charlotte. Or should I say, Madame Charbaneau?" Charlotte's heart skipped a beat as she turned to see Charles standing behind her, looking very fit and as handsome as always, the familiar smile on his face.

"Charles, what are you doing here?" she asked. "I don't remember inviting you."

Charles laughed as he stepped closer, taking her hands in his. "My dear Charlotte, you are such a silly girl. Obviously you don't realize what a small world people like us live in. I am here at the invitation of a friend of your husbands, we went to school together. I'm so sorry I missed your wedding, I hear it was quite lovely."

"Yes, it was," Charlotte replied carefully removing her hands from his. "I didn't know you were over here, I thought you were back home helping father."

"I have been helping, but father wanted me to come here and see what it is you are up to, as you never answer my cards or letters. He has been hearing stories about your band and is quite concerned what people are saying. It isn't proper for you to be traveling around with men like that. Though I must say, I have watched you a few times and your band is pretty good, it's a shame you will have to stop now that you are married, of course."

Charlotte flushed as she stared at her brother. "You have been spying on me?"

"It's not spying. It's protecting you from yourself. You are so naive, even after going to school abroad," Charles shook his head smiling at her.

"I'm not giving up the band, Phillipe loves hearing me sing. So you can just go back home and tell father he doesn't have to worry about me anymore," Charlotte started to push her way past Charles, who grabbed her arm, laughing.

"Such a temper. Have I ever told you how adorable you are when you are mad?"

"Take your hand off me," she replied, yanking her arm away. "You are no longer a guest here, I think you should leave."

"Well, I do believe it's a bit late, as we have already left the dock, see?" Charles pointed to the dock, which was starting to grow smaller as the yacht motored toward the open water. Taking her arm again, he said, "Don't you think it's time you introduce me to your new husband?" Glaring at him, Charlotte allowed herself to be led to where the other guests had gathered.

"Good morning everyone, I'd like to introduce my half- brother, Charles. I hope everyone has a wonderful time. It is a gorgeous day to be out on the water. I see the staff has already been busy with the food and drinks, if you need anything, please let us know. Thank you," The guests raised their glasses in a toast to Charlotte, thanking her. Just then Phillipe strolled up, smiling and shaking hands as people congratulated him on his new bride, and the party on the yacht. Spotting Charlotte, he headed straight to her, beaming with pride.

"There you are, I have been looking all over for you," he said, taking her from Charles and kissing her lightly on the lips. "And who do we have here?" he inquired.

"Phillipe, this is my half- brother Charles. Charles, this is my husband Phillipe."

The two men shook hands, before Phillipe noted, "I am afraid I am at a bit of a loss, Charlotte hasn't told me much about her family."

"Well, we certainly can get to know each other better now that I'm here," Charles smiled.

Phillipe smiled back, "Of course, why don't we get a drink and join the others? Charlotte, shall we?" Together the three walked towards the other guests, who were already enjoying the food and drinks provided.

The drinks flowed as the afternoon wore on. Everyone appeared to be enjoying themselves. Charlotte, who was the only one not drinking, watched as some of the other guests got rather drunk. Mostly, she watched Charles. He was definitely flying high. She wondered if he was just drunk, or stoned, or both. She frowned as she watched him, remembering all too well what happened that night so long ago, she didn't trust him when he was like this. Hopefully, nothing bad would happen, at least she had Phillipe here to protect her, in case he did try something. Hearing someone call her name, she broke out of her reverie, and heading smiling to the guests that were calling to her. If it was one thing she knew how to do, it was play hostess. It was a role she was born into. Everyone was having a good time. She noticed a few couples that had stolen away to the cabins, including a few couples that were married to other people and shook her head. She was sure there would be hell to pay in the morning for a few folks. The evening was setting in and once again she made her way to the deck, standing at the rail, admiring the stars on the water. The wind has picked up and the boat rocked a bit more on the waves, Charlotte rolling with the rhythm. Inhaling deeply, she turned her back to the rail in time to see Charles making his way toward her, carrying two glasses and a bottle of champagne.

"Hey sis, what do you say we have a glass of champagne to toast to your marriage?" he said as he stopped and started pouring a glass for her.

"I don't drink anymore," she said flatly. "And I think you may have had enough for one night, too."

Charles stared at her, "One glass will not hurt you, and who are you to judge how much I've had?" He tried to shove the glass in her hand but she slapped it away.

"I told you, I don't drink, and you are drunk. Please give me the bottle," she reached for the bottle, which Charles tried to wrestle away from her.

Laughing he said, "Maybe that is your problem, you don't drink," leering at her he continued, "I remember a time when you got pretty drunk, you were a lot more fun."

Something inside her snapped, and she slapped him hard across the face, causing him to lose his balance and fall back several steps, the champagne bottle falling to the deck, breaking.

"What the hell!" he yelled as he regained his balance and lunged at her, knocking her to the deck. Straddling her waist he slapped her hard across the face. "You little bitch. Do I need to show you who is in charge?" Grabbing the front of her shirt, he viciously ripped open her blouse. Charlotte yelled and reached on the deck for the broken bottle, grabbing the end and slashing Charles across the face. With a howl of rage, he grabbed her wrist, but before he could do anything else, he felt himself yanked off of her and thrown hard to the deck.

Phillipe yelled as he punched Charles hard in the face. Charles kicked Phillipe viciously in the stomach, sending him backwards a few steps, hunching over from the pain. With a lurch, Charles got to his feet, blood pouring from his face and charged at Phillipe, knocking him back.

"Stop it!" screamed Charlotte as she stood up, still holding the broken bottle. "Stop it!"

Philippe again slammed Charles in the face, who bellowed with rage. Lowering his head, Charles lunged at Phillipe, at the same time the boat rocked with a large wave. Phillipe spun around as he lost his balance, landing face first on Charlotte, the bottle cutting deep into him. Charlotte screamed as she realized what had happened. Phillipe started to get up, holding his stomach as blood poured between his fingers. He looked questioningly at Charlotte, who grabbed and held him, before Charles picked him up, throwing him to the deck, knocking him unconscious.

"Look what you've done!" Charlotte cried.

"Go get help!" Charles grabbed her and shoved her toward the cabins. "Go!" Charlotte turned and holding her blouse together with one hand, the bottle still in her other, she ran screaming to get the captain of the boat, who would have medical training.

When she returned with the captain, and most of the guests who had heard the commotion, Charles was laying on the deck groaning, with no sign of Phillipe.

"Where is he? Where is Phillipe?" she cried, as she stood in the middle of the deck, looking around, seeing nothing but blood. Then she noticed the blood on the railing and screamed, rushing to look over the side of the boat. "Phillipe!" she screamed as she saw his lifeless body floating in the water, getting smaller as the boat sailed away.

Charlotte sat in her cabin, sobbing uncontrollably. The captain had stopped the boat and attended to Charles's wounds while the crew set out in a lifeboat to recover Phillipe's body. Several people had come into the cabin to try and help her, but Charlotte was inconsolable. Little did she know the version of events that Charles was telling. The boat was turned around and heading back to the dock, where the police were waiting, along with several ambulances, having been notified by the captain of the events that had taken place. Suddenly the cabin door opened and Charles came in, locking the door behind him.

"Get out!" screamed Charlotte, "I don't ever want to see you again! You killed my husband!"

Grabbing her hands roughly, Charles glared at his sister. "You listen to me," he hissed. "You have no idea what happened."

"Yes I do, you killed him and threw him overboard!" Charlotte wailed.

Slapping her hard across the face, Charles angrily said, "I did not kill him, you did. Everyone saw you carrying the bottle with blood on it. They recovered his body and found the wound. So, if you don't want to spend the rest of your life in a French prison, you had better listen to me and get your story straight, because right now, you're in big trouble."

"What are you talking about? He was alive, you shoved him onto me, I didn't kill him, it was an accident! You knocked him out and threw him overboard to drown, you bastard!"

"I am telling you, no one will believe you. Phillipe was drunk, he tried to attack you. I tried to protect you and you stabbed him in self- defense. After you ran for help, he got up, stumbled to the rail, but because he was drunk and injured, he lost his balance and fell. End of story. Do you understand?"

"That is not what happened and you know it! You killed him, no one will believe you!"

"That is where you are wrong. You stupid little fool, you haven't learned a damn thing, have you? People saw you with the blood on you, carrying the bottle that killed him. They already believe what I told them, and so will the police. I've contacted our attorney, and father has a plane on the way to get us. This mess you got into is going to cost a lot of money. Phillipe's family is considered nobility here. The locals are going to want your blood for this. You are just a silly, stupid rich girl who plays in a rock band for kicks. Do you really think anyone will believe a word you say? Do you not realize the reputation you have of drugs and orgies with the band? That is what people think of rock and roll for Christ's sake. Once we give our statement, we are getting on the plane and going home. You will be safer there, they can't arrest you."

"I won't do it. I don't care what people think, it's not true, none of it!" Charlotte cried through her tears. "I'm telling them the truth."

"Then you will rot in prison."

Charles continued, "We were on his yacht, he was giving a party and we were cruising the coastline. Phillipe got drunk, attacked. Charlotte, I intervened and he fell on a broken bottle she was holding. I sent her to get the captain for help, and while she was gone, Phillipe attacked me and knocked me down. I should have been able to fend him off, but I had been drinking as well, and so he got the better of me. Next thing I knew, he was standing up, and stumbled to the rail. I don't know if he meant to be sick, but he ended up falling overboard and drowned. Everyone saw Charlotte with the bottle and blood on her and knew she was responsible for his death. I had to make up a story to the police so she wouldn't be arrested, and Father had to pay a lot of money to get us out of there and bring us home. The thanks I get is she tries to say I killed Phillipe."

Graham asked, "If it was self- defense, why not just say so? I'm sorry, but I'm having a hard time buying all this. It sounds a little too convenient."

"There were too many people on the boat who were willing to say she killed him."

"How drunk were all those people? Once again, this sounds like bullshit to me. I'm more willing to believe what Kiki said than what you are trying to make us believe happened," Graham wasn't giving in. "I find it very convenient now that our mother is dead, you blame everything on her."

Charles glared at Graham. "Then you need to think some more of what you do know about your mother. Think of how she was when you were growing up. I'm sure you will remember she was no saint."

"Easy Graham," Emily said as she noted Graham getting angry.

"I'm telling you this is bullshit! Yes, Mom was no saint, and she could pluck your last nerve. God knows we suffered because of her selfishness. But, I know when someone is bullshitting me and I'm telling you it's getting deep in here," Graham glared at Charles as he stood up. "Why don't you try telling the truth for once in your life? You raped a child and murdered her husband, what else have you done?"

Charles also got up, anger flooding his face. "You come into MY home, and accuse me of these things? How dare you! I want you to leave right now! Just because what you heard doesn't match the image of what you want your mother to be is not my fault. I don't have to take this from you, now get out!"

Emily stood up and then, not even knowing where the question came from asked, "Why did you call Mom?"

Charles snapped, "I didn't call her, she called me."

Everyone stopped and stared for a minute before Emily continued, still not knowing where it was coming from, "Where is the letter?" Graham glanced over at Emily, who stayed focused on Charles, "You know what I'm talking about, where is the letter?"

"What letter?"

Emily decided to run with whatever was guiding her, "it was from her mother. You took it. Where is it?"

"That letter is private, it is not for you."

"It was her letter, and since she is dead, it belongs to us. Now hand over the letter," Emily held out her hand.

"What did she tell you about the letter?" Charles had paled slightly.

Sweating and praying she was right, Emily answered, "She said it explained everything. Everything you did and how that letter was going to put you away for the rest of your life. I said, hand it over."

"NO!" thundered Charles. "I will destroy it, you will never get it!" Graham and Emily could see that Charles was beginning to lose his sanity.

Nervously, Charlotte pulled into the parking lot by the trail head. It was still early, and there were no other cars around. "That would change," she thought, as the temperatures were supposed to go up later this afternoon. People would probably want to get their walk or run in before it got too hot. This week was going to be a scorcher, considering how early it was in the spring. That was the way the weather was in Virginia. One week it was freezing and snow, and then the next week it was like summertime. You just never knew what the weather would do.

Getting out of the car, Charlotte grabbed her walking stick, and locked the car. She was planning on a shorter hike than she normally took, just something to clear her head before she met Charles in town later this morning. She thought back to their phone conversation, he had seemed quite surprised to hear from her, and a little guarded. She guessed she would be the same if he called her out of the blue, insisting they needed to meet and discuss some things. She knew she would need to be on her toes for this one, he wasn't going to like what she had to say, and knowing how bad he could be if he was angered, it could get ugly. That was the reason she decided to meet him in a public place, she felt safer with other people around. Then again, there had been other people on the yacht and look how that turned out. She had to stop thinking like a victim, she decided. Think about everything he had done and how he had ruined her life. It was time to stand up for herself once and for all. And, it was time he paid for the things he had done.

Walking quickly down the trail, her mind on the past, she barely registered all the beauty surrounding her. Before she knew it, she was walking up a hill, feeling her breathing getting more difficult. "I really need to get in better shape," she thought, "I remember when I could do this hill without even breathing hard. Maybe it was the humidity." She bet there would be thunderstorms this afternoon. Real ones, not just the one she expected from Charles.

Stopping to rest for a moment, she surveyed her surroundings and noticed a group of daffodils along the trail. "I wonder how they got there," she thought. Maybe there had been a house here long ago, the only reminder being the daffodils that survived. Maybe someday she would do some research of the area, see what used to be here before the railway owned it. She continued her walk, knowing once she reached the top it was a nice downhill to the creek. She loved walking along the creek side, it was so calming listening to the water. Normally, she would bring something to eat and have a picnic by the water, but today she wouldn't have time, so she didn't bring anything. Still, she would stop and rest, then head back to meet Charles.

Reaching the creek side trail, Charlotte slowed her pace. Stopping at her favorite spot, she sat on a rock by the water, letting the sounds of the water splashing over the rocks soothe her nerves. She could hear the small waterfall a few feet away, and the occasional splash as something jumped in the water. She sighed, wishing her mind could always be this serene. Lately, it seemed that her thoughts were more and more chaotic. She blamed most of that on Jonathan and his ever present need for money. At least she put an end to that, though she wasn't naive enough to think he wouldn't try again. She just needed to stand her ground. For too many years she had let him dominate her, feeling guilty for bringing him into the world without a father, only because she wanted someone to love and need her. Babies were great that way, they relied on you for everything, and didn't ask for much other than to be fed, held and have their diapers changed. They were like puppies, totally dependent and adoring. Unlike puppies, however, babies grew up and became spoiled brats.

Glancing at her watch, she realized she needed to start heading back. Leaning on the walking stick, she pushed herself up to her feet, dusted off her pants, and stifled a scream when she saw the man standing behind her. He just stared at her, not saying anything. He was older, but soon she recognized the stance, and the smile that crept on his face.

"Charles! You almost gave me a heart attack! What are you doing here? We are supposed to meet at the cafe," Charlotte had a hand at her heart, which was still racing.

"Hello Charlotte. You're looking well. I almost didn't recognize you with your short hair. You had such glorious hair. You should never have cut it." They stared at each other, neither moving.

"Yeah, well, it was too much to take care of, plus in this heat, short hair is much cooler. You look very well yourself, you still look the same. But really, how did you get here? Don't tell me you are still following me around after all these years."

Charles laughed. "You haven't changed a bit, silly girl. Of course I'm following you today. You ignore me for forty years, then call out of the blue and want to meet? Did you really think I'd show up at some cafe in town to discuss family business in public?"

Uneasiness setting in, Charlotte reminded herself to stay strong, she had to do this, she just had to. Holding tightly to the walking stick she replied "Well then, since you're here, I guess you want to know why I called."

Charles just stared at her, raising an eyebrow quizzically, waiting for her to continue.

"I was going through a box of letters and found one from my mother. What is weird is that I don't remember seeing it before, and had never

read it."

Charles continued to stare at her, "And?"

Pulling out the letter, she showed it to him. "It was written shortly before she died. I should have received it while I was at school, but I never did."

"What is your point? You drag me down here for some letter written decades ago? What could it possible matter today?" Charles was clearly getting annoyed.

Taking a deep breath, and getting a bit angry herself, she continued, "The point is, my mother knew you raped me. She believed in me. She knew you were lying. She said she confronted you about it, which of course you denied, trying to blame me, but she stuck up for me."

Grabbing the letter from her hands, Charles replied angrily, "You dragged me down here for that old crap? Who are you trying to fool here? You were a tramp! You paraded around half naked, flaunting your body in front of me, rubbing up against me any chance you got! What did you expect would happen, huh? YOU, were the one that was asking for it, then you get drunk and throw yourself at me, what did you expect? You got what you wanted and then you try to blame me! You are nothing but a whore!"

"I was twelve! You were the brother that I adored, I looked up to you! I wasn't interested in you sexually, I didn't even know what sex was until you took away my virginity! You ruined my life!" Charlotte fought back tears as she yelled at her brother.

"Ruined your life? Give me a break! Get over yourself. You are nothing but a spoiled, narcissistic, crazy whore. You've spent your entire life catering to your own desires, and then try to blame me?" Charles

grabbed her by the arm. "We have had this conversation enough times already, I'm done listening to you whine about your damn virginity! It wasn't like you weren't screwing your way around Europe. You didn't care about it then, did you?"

Charlotte tried to yank her arm away, but his grip was too strong. "Let go of me!"

Pulling her closer to his face, he growled, "We are going to settle this once and for all. So tell me, what else did your mother say in her letter?"

Panic was starting to set in, but she responded, "She told me that after confronting you, that is when she started getting ill. How you went from barely talking to her, to suddenly being at her beck and call, bringing her special drinks and food, even if she didn't want any. You forced her to eat and drink them. She felt you were poisoning her, but of course father wouldn't believe anything she said."

"That is ridiculous!" Charles tightened his grip on her arm. Shaking the letter in her face before stuffing it in his pocket, he continued "Your mother was a crazy loon, and so are you. You both should have just listened to what the men told you and you would have been much better off. Women like you two don't get that men are in charge. You may think that you are with your whore ways, but you aren't. You are too stupid to do anything but take care of a man. That is what your mother forgot. She forgot her place, and so did you."

"I believe her! You killed my mother, and then you killed Phillipe! You have destroyed everything that ever mattered to me! All because I wouldn't let you touch me again. It killed you to think of me with another man, didn't it? I bet it would kill you to know how much better they were than you! You are nothing but a child rapist, and a murderer! I'm going to see that you get what is coming to you, you have gotten *away with too much all these years, it's time you get what you deserve! I am taking the letter to the police! There is no statute of limitation for murder. Do you know what happens to child rapists in prison? I'm sure you will be very popular."*

With a roar, Charles threw Charlotte to the ground, "You bitch, how dare you say that to me!" Pinning her to the ground, he slapped her across the face. "You are nothing but a crazy bitch! I'll show you who is in charge, you will never even think of going to the police with your lies!" he yelled, punching her in the face.

Charlotte's mind reeled with the pain. "God, he was strong," she thought. Grabbing the walking stick she brought it up and swinging it as hard as she could, she connected it with his head. Screaming with pain and rage, Charles grabbed the stick and brought it down on her head, breaking the stick. Her mind spun as she drifted into unconsciousness, fortunately no longer aware as Charles grabbed the rock next to her and furiously and repeatedly brought it down on her head.

"Hand it over, the police have already been told and they are on their way as we speak. Give up, you are going to pay for what you've done," Emily was so scared she was shaking, but her voice remained steady.

Charles suddenly exploded, "I told her it was all her fault, I told her she would still be alive if she listened! SHE NEVER LISTENED! Her mother deserved to die; she was trying to frame me. Do you know what would have happened to me if anyone listened to her, and believed I raped her precious daughter? I had to stop her. I knew they would never detect the arsenic. Like

Phillipe, it was almost too easy. If Charlotte hadn't rejected me, he would still be alive. What was the big deal? She was putting out for every man she could, why not me? He had to be the big hero and try to save her. Serves him right. And Charlotte? If she didn't decide to drag all this up, she'd still be alive, but no, she wanted justice! I'll give you justice!" Graham and Emily were stunned and couldn't react as Charles suddenly reached into his desk and pulled out a gun. Emily screamed as she heard the click of the safety being released, and Graham lunged forward towards Charles.

Parker and Kenny drove up to the estate and saw Graham's car in the driveway. "Looks like we aren't the only ones wanting a talk with Charles," Parker noted. Getting out, they headed up the steps when they heard a scream, followed by a gunshot. Quickly drawing their weapons, they kicked in the door, yelling "Police!" From the library, they heard Emily yell, "In here, hurry!"

Rushing into the library, Parker and Kenny saw Emily in tears, standing next to Graham, who appeared dazed. On the floor was Charles, a bullet hole at his temple. Parker holstered his weapon and kneeled down to take a pulse, knowing it was already too late. Looking up at Kenny, he said "Call it in and secure the scene, he's gone."

Later, as Graham and Emily prepared to leave, Emily put her hands in her pockets. Surprised, she pulled out an envelope addressed to her mother. Confused, she showed it to Graham.

"How did you get that?" he asked.

"I have no idea," she got chills as she opened it and read:

"Dear Emily, Thank you. Love Mom."

ABOUT THE AUTHOR

Susan M Viemeister lives on a small farm in Virginia, along with her husband, dogs, a cat that thinks he's a dog, and one very old horse. She and her husband are avid mountain bikers, and can occasionally be spotted on the local trails. Susan is currently working on her next novel.

Made in the USA
Charleston, SC
26 October 2016